Snow is Silent

BENJAMÍN PRADO

Snow is Silent

Translated by Sam Richard

faber and faber

First published in Spain in 2000
as *La nieve está vacía* by Espasa Narrativa
This translation first published in the United Kingdom in 2005
by Faber and Faber Limited
3 Queen Square London WC1N 3AU

Typeset by Faber and Faber Ltd
Printed in England by Mackays of Chatham, plc

The right of Sam Richard to be identified as translator of this work
has been asserted in accordance with Section 77 of the Copyright,
Designs and Patents Act 1988

This publication has been translated with aid from the General Department
for Books, Archives and Libraries of the Spanish Ministry of Education,
Culture and Sports

A CIP record for this book
is available from the British Library

ISBN 0–571–22339–7

2 4 6 8 10 9 7 5 3 1

SNOW IS SILENT

One of Us Three

It had been raining very shortly before, so the city still presented an odd combination of wet pavements and stifling heat when one of us three set off from his home last night, at about 11.30, to kill Laura Salinas. For the moment, I can't reveal his name or which of the three is me. How will I manage it? Easy: I'll tell you everything that happened in the third person, that way when I say 'Iker Orbáiz lit a cigarette', 'Ángel Biedma thought back again to what it was he'd been doing at the time of the crime' or 'Alcaén Sánchez would have given his life to buy her that house', you'll never be sure if I'm talking about one of the other two or if, in fact, I'm referring to myself.

Those are the rules; if they're not to your liking, it's better that you leave now, forget about Laura Salinas, go back to minding your own business and stop wasting my time. To those of you, however, who do decide to stay and listen to this story, let me give you a piece of advice: first, you are only readers, not detectives, so don't try to draw conclusions or discover anything for yourselves; second, in this story things work the opposite way round to normal, because the characters are real and the narrator is invented; he's not a man of flesh and blood, but an invisible being, pure fiction. Trying to link me with any of the main characters will get you nowhere, for two reasons: I have rearranged events as would an omnipresent narrator – as if I had been there on all occasions – and this is neither my voice nor my usual way of speaking; I've confined myself, more or less, to writing in the style of a detective novel, so rest assured that whether we meet in a bank or in a grocer's, in a lift or a chemist's you will never recognise me, not in this book, nor out there; whether you're seeing me for the first time or if you're the people who live next door it will make no difference. Like I said, for now, I'm an invisible being.

There is something I do want to tell you before I start though, and that's whichever one of us left home at about 11.30 last night to kill Laura Salinas, that person was a broken man, a man with no way out. He took slow, faltering steps, as though emerging from a battlefield, as though fleeing from bombardments, from ruined buildings, from Death, whose thousand red mouths gape from the bodies of the fallen. As for his eyes, they had a fevered, shattered look. Had you seen him for yourselves that night, I'm sure he wouldn't have seemed very dangerous, just someone very frightened.

And it's true that he was afraid; it was the fear he had always had of dark parks and silent streets, the fear that all empty settings provoke precisely because they are empty: the disquiet of their lines of motionless cars, of the dogs that don't bark, the people you can't see, the locked-up shops.

He wondered if his pain would ever end. That sharp, all-encompassing pain. That sinuous pain in the shape of a snake. Perhaps he would manage to recover, he told himself, maybe it was only a matter of time: 'In a few days from now, this will have gone away along with everything else, just like when the snow melts, with tracks left by wolves.'

I'm going to tell you what had to happen for that man to reach that state, for him to wander the city alone, in pursuit of Laura Salinas, trying to imagine her killer's bad dreams.

2

The Great Deal

It was all around him, and it drove him crazy. He could feel it in the smooth touch of the banister, its perfect lines and creamy finish; he could hear it in the elegant creak of the stairs, sense it in the green or red thickness underfoot: here were expensive carpets, the finest wood. Alcaén Sánchez paused by one of the windows and took a last look at the garden, at the small fountain, the swing beneath the trees. Then he turned back to the other man, accepted the business card offered him, and walked calmly towards the door, pausing to study again certain features of the architecture – the ceiling mouldings, the doorways – attempting to convey in his every gesture the impression that he was a man of means, well accustomed to luxury and wealth; someone just back from two weeks on his yacht.

The truth is he was not really sure why he went to such lengths, why for years now he had been visiting houses he could never afford. Perhaps it was a way of raising his own hopes, of allowing himself to envisage a bright and comfortable future, free from worry or hardship; or perhaps it was nothing more than a game that allowed him to pretend, for a few minutes, while he dealt with the estate agents, that he really was the man he went disguised as – a confident, worldly guy whose reputation was based, above all, on an optimistic nature and a bank balance that ran to eight figures. He should have known that to play games is dangerous, that there is no game in which you have nothing to lose. At the time, though, this was something he had yet to learn.

That visit, however, seemed to him not quite the same as the others. The usual things had happened, of course: his portrayal of the prospective client turning up for a Saturday morning appointment in a combination of expensive suit and designer polo shirt, a sign as much of his free-and-easy manner as of his wealth; there had also been the salesman's initial suspicion, the practised gaze that tried to value Alcaén Sánchez, relate him to a specific sum of money, and that, a little later, when the potential impostor had let slip a couple of satisfactory details and begun to seem real, was replaced by a flow of syrupy words and a wide, promotional smile.

'Here we have a small private library,' the swindling estate agent was saying, 'with an exquisite view of the garden. The display cabinets are real oak. A lovely quiet corner, wouldn't you agree? Perfect for forgetting all about life's little worries. Inside here is a drinks cabinet. And that door leads through to one of the bedrooms.'

Alcaén remained silent, while seeming to carefully ponder every inch of the room and each one of the salesman's remarks.

'Hmm, there wouldn't be space for even a third of our books in here,' he replied eventually, in the tone of one not used to beating about the bush. 'As for the drinks cabinet, in my family we're all abstemious. Though I do agree – it is a nice spot.'

5

The word 'abstemious' earned him a thousand points of esteem with the salesman, who must have considered it irrefutable proof of Alcaén's class, the telling detail that confirmed his favourable first impression, for he spread his arms in an almost priestly gesture and gave him a gaze full of veneration. He was mistaken. The reality was that if what Alcaén had drunk the night before had been petrol, it would have been enough to fuel a car's journey from Cádiz to New Delhi.

He was remembering all this on the bus taking him back to the centre, but, most of all, he remembered his surprise on finding out how much the house cost. Caught up with that figure, he barely noticed how the wide, immaculate streets of the private housing development gave way first to wooded land, then to a motorway, before becoming the outskirts of the city. It was a December morning; the shop windows were decked out as splendidly as wedding cakes, and people were walking about with colourful packages and holding children by the hand. Probably none of them were ready to be better than they were, but they were certainly ready to enjoy a great couple of weeks, and so the atmosphere seemed charged with that propensity for happiness normally referred to as Christmas spirit.

Fifty million pesetas. That was how much the house cost, an amount that seemed to him both small and yet beyond his means. It was undoubtedly a good price, but could *he* even allow himself to dream of affording it. Of course not. Though maybe if he sold his apartment, received an advance at work, did a second job in the evenings, asked his bank for a loan . . . He went on speculating: he pictured his life in that house with such clarity that he could even replace himself with the cheerful, well-to-do figure the unctuous estate agent had glimpsed a short while before, in the distance, in the future, converted already into that residence's new owner, when Alcaén had said to him:

'Well, fifty million is quite an investment. Though by no means excessive.'

A look of pure pleasure creased the salesman's face – or perhaps it was uncertainty that caused this, an effort intended, in some way, to transform his features into those of someone twice as sincere, more worthy of complete confidence. It was an expression that tried to say: 'Trust me. It's a great deal. I would never cheat you.'

The bus reached its destination. For a while Alcaén wandered around, looking at the shops, the kiosks, the fruit and vegetable stores; he checked the menus and prices of a couple of restaurants and, in the end, having decided against any unnecessary spending, he bought some apples and set off in the direction of the Sívori Bar, where he spent most of his evenings. He could eat the apples and drink a few beers, and, at some point, he'd be joined by Iker Orbáiz, his best friend. Alcaén wanted to tell him about the house and, as he walked, he prepared the best way to broach the subject. He could practically see him there: Iker making up one of his strange fables, the others listening attentively, appearing to find something of personal relevance in one of those tales in which, for example, a man embarks on a one-way journey lead-ing to madness and disaster, after waking up one morning and realising he never appears in his own dreams; or in which a woman who is about to die confesses to her children that her entire life – and by extension theirs – has been based on a lie: she seduced her husband by means of a subterfuge, by pretending to be a different person. Alcaén, that house for sale coursing through his veins, has not followed with his usual attention the progress of these stories still in the process of construction; and, as soon as Iker stops talking, Alcaén looks him in the eyes and says:

'You know what? I think I'm about to get myself into a fine mess.'

I won't say yet how much truth that phrase contained, without his knowing it. But I suppose we'd all agree that our lives would be that much better if only we could distinguish such phrases from certain others: if only we could realise when something is only a figure of speech and when it represents a prophecy. Because if that were possible, none of this would ever have happened.

3

The Man Who Never Appeared in His Own Dreams

'Imagine you could go back to a day in your life,' said Iker, 'and could choose a particular moment, just one, from which to start again. Which one would you . . ?'

Ángel Biedma raised his hand, to stop him, with a commanding gesture.

'Hang on a minute,' he said. 'Would I know what was going to happen to me after that? Because that's very important. In fact, that'd change everything.'

'After what?'

'Suppose I'm able to go back to, say, June 1975, when I had that traffic accident in Barcelona. The one I told you about, remember?'

'Yeah, I remember: a van cut into your lane, you slammed on the brakes; it didn't do much good, though – it'd been raining and the road surface was wet.'

'Right. Well, my question is, if I could go back to that morning, would I calmly sit myself down in a bar on the Ramblas to enjoy a few cool drinks, and say to myself: "I have no intention of getting into that car, because the last time I did I ended up with two broken legs."?'

Ángel's eyes glinted, as if wisdom were something metallic.

'No, of course not. It's a case of having the same life over again, only this time with some bits taken away and some bits added. What the man wants to find out is where he started to go wrong, and why. Do you understand? It's not a question of magic, but of finding an explanation.'

'Let's see if I've got this right: a man wakes up one morning and starts thinking about the dream he had the night before and which, as always, he remembers with absolute clarity. Recalling some of the stories that passed through his mind while he was asleep, and relating them to each other, he suddenly makes a worrying discovery: he realises that he never appears in any of his own dreams. That's how your story begins, isn't it?'

'Correct.'

'All right. I have a question: why does he find that so frightening? You'll need a valid reason. Why does that sudden realisation turn his life upside down? Perhaps it'd be better if something more . . . I don't know . . . more extraordinary happened to him.'

'There's no need. It's as though that discovery were a small light shining into a large empty room. Do you follow me? It's simply the end of the rope, the mouth of the abyss.'

'And it turns out that at the end of the rope there's a noose.'

'Exactly. At the end of the rope there's always a noose. That's precisely what the story is about.'

'Why didn't he realise that sooner?'

'Realise what? How wretched he is? Perhaps he never looked into that corner of his life before. When he does, the floodgates open. Isn't truth supposed to destroy liars?

Why not include in that definition people who lie to themselves?'

'Why, then, doesn't he just keep on looking the other way? It'd be easy, wouldn't it? He could just step back from that abyss you mentioned, not tug on that rope.'

'No, I don't think he'd be able to. He needs to understand what has happened to him. That's why he wonders at what point he took a wrong turn, and he dreams of returning to that moment, setting things right. He needs to find that day.'

'Even if that means losing everything he has?'

'What are you talking about? This has nothing to do with losing or gaining anything, it's about discovering something.'

'What's the difference?'

'The same as that between an archaeologist and a grave robber.'

Ángel and Iker carried on in this vein for some time, while Alcaén waited for the right moment to tell them about the house he'd found and about his plans for the future. He looked around him: the Sívori had a peaceful ambience, a bar of dark wood, two or three mirrors and a dartboard, five dozen more-or-less exotic bottles lined up along its shelves and, above all, that combination of green lamps and red velvet armchairs that makes the men who go there to spend their money and flee their families feel comfortable. On the bathroom door there was a photograph of T. S. Eliot, which was one of Iker's classic coded jokes: if you remove the 'S', and read backwards, T. S. Eliot becomes 'toilet'.

'Listen, you two, I've something to tell you,' Alcaén began. But at that moment, Gloria, the owner of the Sívori, came up to their table with three tankards of beer.

'Here's that next round you were about to order,' she said.

'We were? How do you know?'

'Cos this is a bar, not a library. People come here to drink and leave me their salaries. The rest is none of my business.'

She was about forty years old, with intense green eyes, a firm figure and, in general, the kind of defiant beauty that suggested a difficult past as well as the determination to defend herself tooth and nail against anyone who thought she could be taken advantage of again. Rumour had it she came from an upper-class background; had spent ten years married to a powerful man, and had bought the Sívori in a fit of rage, after her husband told her he was leaving her. 'I've met someone else,' he confessed to her one night. 'I know I'm behaving like a bastard, that you don't deserve this. I wish it'd never happened, I feel awful, but that's the way it is, I need a fresh start' . . . The next morning Gloria went to the bank, withdrew all their savings, and left her husband a note: 'This is so you really can, like you said, make a fresh start.'

'But it's clear there must've been more to it than that,' Iker would always say, whenever the subject was mentioned. 'Why didn't he try to get his money back? Why didn't he get his lawyers on to her? If Gloria did buy the Sívori with what they had in the bank that means we're talking millions; I reckon twenty-five, thirty million, maybe a lot more. What was it she knew that could keep him at bay? And there's another question we ought to ask: who was she before we met her? Why didn't she go back to her upper-class family? Instead of which, she set up this business. That's the key to it, the two questions you need to ask in order to know a person: where they come from, and what happened there.'

'Maybe this was just a stepping stone,' said Ángel Biedma, 'a first step on the path to a better life.'

'Only things didn't at all turn out the way she'd hoped they would, not by a long shot.'

'No, of course they didn't. At some stage she must have thought this was just a beginning, but this turned out to be it.'

'Which leaves Gloria feeling tremendously bitter towards the swine who left her. In fact, one of the bottles there behind the bar doesn't contain what it says on the label, it's poison, of the kind that needs time to take effect. What d'you think? She keeps it up there in case her husband comes in to the Sívori one day? Wouldn't that be a wonderful revenge! The perfect crime: two weeks later the police find the body at his home; they can tell he's been murdered, but they've no way of finding out who did it, what the motive was, or where he had that fatal drink. Besides, even if they did ever suspect the truth, how would they prove it?'

'So in the end she kills him? Hmm, dunno, strikes me as too much of a coincidence, him walking into the Sívori.'

'Actually, it doesn't matter. All we know is that Gloria has that fatal dose of arsenic ready, that it's there, a menacing presence. As though the mere fact of having it could alter her past, change it for the better.'

Alcaén was always there on these occasions, sitting with Iker and Ángel, listening to them piece together the story about Gloria, or the one about the man who never appeared in his own dreams, or the mother who reveals to her children that their life is based on a lie. In fact, they had become friends in the first place because one night two years earlier, he'd approached them as they were inventing one of their stories and had shown such interest in what they were saying that they had ended up inviting him to join them. In the course of the introductions they learnt that Alcaén worked in an insurance company, while he learnt that Iker Orbáiz wanted to be a writer and that Ángel Biedma was a doctor; that both of them liked beer and books and talking non-stop – a locking of intellectual horns, from which one got ideas for his stories and the other, the infinite pleasure of two or three hours of conversation. To his two new friends, Alcaén at once became something of great value: he became their audience.

He clearly recalled that first meeting: as he walked over to their table, he'd had the feeling that he recognised the scene and, even, that he knew what each of them was going to say next; he had that disturbing feeling that makes us think the logical order of things has suddenly been reversed and that memories precede events. One day, a long time afterwards, he told this to Iker, who then began to write a story in which a man remembers Prague despite never having been there; if he closes his eyes he sees St Vitus's Cathedral, the streets of Malá Strana, the green tiled roofs of St Nicholas's Church, the statues on Charles Bridge; if he searches his memory, he remembers a visit to the house of the poet Vladimir Holan, by the river; a small restaurant open near Hradcany Square; the morning he visited the Jewish cemetery – he went there in a red bus, the ground was covered in ivy, Kafka's grave looked exactly the same as all the other graves. But there's something else: for some reason, in each one of those episodes he always sees a small boy dressed in white, some distance away – as if on the other side of a street – but whose strong, regular features, and blue, slightly oriental eyes, he can make out clearly. Who is he? Where do they know each other from? What is the boy waiting for? When Christmas comes, the man decides to take a trip to Prague. For the first few days, everything has the immutability expected of the familiar, the sense of a return: the House of the Two Suns still stands on Jan Neruda Street, the House of the Golden Serpent on Karlova Street; Czech beer retains its bitter, unmistakable taste; five minutes away from Old Town Square there are bars where you eat standing up, cheap establishments where people form long queues to get a plateful of kidneys, a drink, a dessert. As the days go by, though, the things he does also take on a new quality, a kind of vivid realism which, little by little, gradually replaces what had previously only been a sense of premonition, just as, on meeting an acquaintance we haven't seen in a long while, the evidence of the person before us slowly discredits the image we had in mind, colonising it inch by inch until it disappears. Whatever it was, by the time his holiday draws to a close he has almost forgotten what brought him to Prague, or at least, he now takes his impulse to have been some form of absurd superstition. On the last night, however, as he leaves a restaurant in the Old City he sees, standing by a lamp post on the other side of the street, someone he thinks is the young blue-eyed boy, with his beautiful Slavic features and his white outfit; he starts towards the boy but, at that very instant, he remembers something more: the traffic lights on red, the sound of an engine, the yellow-painted van; he turns, like the first time, but again he is too slow; he turns the other way, only to see the van coming straight at him.

Iker promised Alcaén that when the book was published the story would be dedicated to him. It was a promise to which Alcaén attached the rather exaggerated importance those without great ambitions attribute to small events – those people who, deep down, do not so much want to make their lives better as to make them more bearable. It may also have been that Alcaén recognised something of himself in the fatalism of the story, since he was the sort of man who sees a bad omen in nearly everything; for whom a beach implies a drowning, a knife means a scar – by the same logic that the rest of us, when we see a bed, presume a body lying down.

Was that also the way he thought about the house that he was, at last, going to tell Iker and Ángel about? Most probably, it was. If Laura Salinas had not got in the way,

Alcaén would, most probably, merely have acted in character yet again, feigning a couple of punches and then giving up. But how could he know what awaited him? How could he have predicted what awaited all three of them and what they would become? A human being is like a sheet of ice: you never know what lies below the surface, what freezing waters, what dark abyss, what monsters of the deep. Which is why, when he bit into one of his apples and began to tell his story, not one of them noticed anything unusual; not one of them sensed the danger coming. Instead, there they calmly remained, sitting back in the red armchairs of the Sívori, drinking their beers as if it were a night on which nothing bad was going to begin.

4

At Times, Money Cuts Like a Knife

When he phoned the estate agency from his office a couple of days later, Alcaén Sánchez completely agreed with Ángel and Iker, who'd told him his idea about buying that house was absurd, an ambition well beyond his means.

'It's a nice dream,' Iker had said. 'But it's someone else's.'

Nevertheless, he did make that second phone call and arrange another appointment. Why? Did he still see a remote chance of borrowing enough money, or did he just want to see the house with its garden one more time? In fact, he waited for the next weekend with great anticipation, with such intense longing that the hours at work became interminable; it seemed like torture dealing with the company's clients, all those drivers who came to him with problems and disasters, many of them intent on cheating the insurance company, ready to make up the most far-fetched lies so that their policy would cover the costs of their accidents and breakdowns.

'No, I didn't crash into the tree, the tree crashed onto my car; it was blown over by the wind.'

'Of course I swerved into the opposite lane, but only to avoid the boy in the middle of the motorway. A paralysed boy, in a wheelchair.'

The company, for its part, derived all its prosperity from a firm and incorruptible lack of principles whose ten commandments could be summed up in one alone: Thou shalt not pay. So, in most cases, the tricks and excuses proved superfluous – those who'd had accidents paid their repair bills and kept up their premiums, but afterwards went round the bars in their neighbourhood lying like demons, telling everyone how they'd put the wind up those crooks at the insurance company, how they'd watched them shake with fear and anger when they threatened to report them, to provoke a scandal; when they yelled in their faces that they'd sink their company, that they'd find a way to ruin them, have them sent to prison. In actual fact, most of them would've been unable to find a Greek in *The Iliad*, but talking big made them feel better, less vulnerable, a little stronger.

Alcaén had two jobs at the office: in the morning he had to attend to claims from clients, and in the afternoon, in the hour before close of business, he was in charge of the day's takings – counting the money that for a variety of reasons had collected in the safe and that he tallied up before putting it back, where it remained overnight until first thing in the morning when the director handed it over to a pair of security guards who took it to the bank in an armoured van.

While he awaited the Saturday, his mechanical existence proved harder to bear than normal; he found it difficult to overcome a succession of days that were both empty and onerous, each one like the next, days that clung to the skin like wet clothes in a storm. 'If only I could buy that house,' he kept telling himself; and behind that phrase lay all the personal changes he could imagine: no more alcohol or easy women, no more lounging around in the Sívori; he'd read the books Iker and Ángel discussed instead of settling for hearing them talked about; he'd push for promotion at work . . . Had it not been for the appearance of Laura Salinas, perhaps it would have been just another one of his impossible desires, a hope rapidly discredited by reality and, as such, harmless, for a dream only becomes dangerous when there's no other dream to take its place: you open a bottle and when there's no more fizz, you open the next. Except that things worked precisely the opposite way round. Simple as that. Don't tell me you don't know what I'm talking about. Some of you are like that, I bet: mediocre, cowardly types, the sort who never make a move for fear of leaving something behind; who hide in their clean consciences, in their sheltered lives, who know how to construct shields to keep them apart from the battle, bridges to distance them from the river. Does my saying this bother you? I don't care; think what you want about me; you couldn't hurt my feelings, not even with a cannon; you haven't suffered enough to know how to cause me pain. And, in any case, that's not what we're here to talk about, so we'd better get back to the only thing that concerns us: the story.

When Saturday came, Alcaén took a bus to the housing development where the property was located, still wondering if some alternative were possible. Perhaps he could offer the estate agency a deal, arrange to pay the fifty million in instalments, maybe give them his apartment and savings to start with, then put his signature to notes, agree to clauses, sign away his salary for life: he earned 200,000 pesetas a month; if he could live on 25,000, which would leave a little over two million a year, which, multiplied by twenty . . . He winced in disgust. 'Shut up,' he told himself; 'stop having these stupid thoughts,' as if addressing someone else. He then started to read the newspaper: a man called Jean-Claude Roman was on trial in France for murdering his wife, two children, parents and dog when he feared they would finally discover that his entire life had been one gigantic hoax and that he was neither a doctor nor an employee of the World Health Organisation – as he had led everyone to believe for the past eighteen years – only a lunatic who had never even finished his second year at university; who every morning left his house bound for a non-existent office, got in his car and drove to a car park where he let the working hours go by and invented congresses and business meetings, names of colleagues, bosses and clients, invented anecdotes about his day at the office which he told his family when he got home. According to the newspaper, it all started when Roman failed his first exams in the Faculty of Medicine, then tried to hide his failure as a student; from that point on, little by little, the lies led him on to others, and these on to ones that were even bigger and more complex, ever less manageable and ever more dangerous.

Alcaén wondered whether Iker Orbáiz already knew that story, whether perhaps it was the source of inspiration for his story about the woman who tells her children that their life has always been a sham. He kept the article to show it that evening to Iker and Ángel Biedma. Then he turned to the sports pages.

On reaching his stop, he made the final adjustments to his disguise – the businessman's suit, the pale-green polo shirt – lit a thin black cigarillo, swapped the real Alcaén's walk, always somewhat weary and effortful, for one that was more dynamic, more confident, and then knocked on the door of the house, expecting the salesman to come out and welcome him, expecting to be met with the same obsequious gestures and contorted courtesy. But the figure who appeared in the doorway was Laura Salinas and, instantly, the moment he set eyes on her, Alcaén felt his heart first stop then cleave in two, like an apple sliced in half by a butcher's knife. Was that how it happened – so swiftly, so undeniably? No one can say. People never know what happened, only what they remember.

In any event, what was seen by Alcaén that morning was not simply a woman of average height with feline, ochre eyes – eyes that were beautiful and enigmatic, reminiscent of a plant that concealed in the earth a great root; a slim woman wearing dark lipstick, a shade between brown and cherry; with very short chestnut hair, pale skin that nevertheless had about it a hidden, somewhat golden light, akin to that of coins glinting in the depths of a fountain. What was seen by Alcaén was a fragile body that would arch at a caress, hands made to be held at the cinema or in the park, a mouth in the likeness of a small, as yet undiscovered tropical fruit; what was seen was a

lifetime at her side, a life which, incongruously, he pretended to remember bit by bit as they went round the
house, as she showed him the shower from which he had
so often seen her emerge naked, her beautiful breasts
swaying hypnotically with every step, droplets of water
lingering about her shoulders; the blue sofa on which
some nights they made love after getting home from a
restaurant or party; the wardrobe where he had once . . .

'Señor Sánchez? Are you feeling OK?'

Alcaén was startled to hear her voice. 'I'm sorry; it's
just that you're so unbearably pretty, so pure,' he would
have liked to have said to her. But, unfortunately, he was
not that kind of man.

'Oh, yes . . . it's only a . . .'

'Don't worry. That's fine. I was just saying the house
runs on natural gas and that the heating . . .' she stopped
and gave him a penetrating look – trying, it seemed, to
make him out. 'That often happens to me too, you know.
All of a sudden . . .' she gestured with her hand, '. . .
you're in one place and your thoughts in another.'

'Or in several all at once.'

'Yes, or even several all at once. Then all the different
places suddenly merge back into one, leaving no trace,
like fragments of a drop of mercury.'

'Right, it's . . . It's normal. Well, what I mean is . . . it's
not normal, it's strange, but it's also . . . Or rather . . .'
The girl laughed on seeing Alcaén tie himself up in knots,
and to Alcaén that laughter's sweet timbre seemed the
most wonderful sound he had ever heard; it seemed to
him that within it was all the music in the world: Brahms

23

laughter, Mozart laughter, Billie Holliday laughter, Elvis laughter, Beatles laughter, Bob Dylan laughter. It seemed to him, too, that something so perfect could never become his. After all, who was he to expect such a thing?

'Anyway, Señor Sánchez, that's everything now. Unless you wanted to have another quick look at the garden. Or anywhere else, for that matter.'

'The garden?'

'Perhaps you'd like to see the garage again. You'll have noticed it only has parking space for two cars.'

'No, I don't think I . . .' He thrust his hand into the pocket of his jacket and, as soon as his fingers closed round the packet of thin black cigarillos, he appeared to pull himself together suddenly, realising that he was behaving as if he were merely himself. '. . . Do you smoke?' he said rather brusquely, taking out the cigarettes.

For a moment the girl observed him with caution, surprised perhaps by the strange turn in the conversation; yet Alcaén could sense that she was somehow pleased by that sudden extravagance.

'I do, actually; but not now, thank you. What are they, menthol?'

'That's right. Chic rubbish, you know the kind of thing – gives you an elegant green cancer.'

It was a phrase he had uttered dozens of times, on each of his visits to houses that were for sale. In fact, he considered it one of the central pieces in his repertoire.

'In that case,' said the woman, 'I will have one.'

'As for the garden, I think you're right: I would like to have another look at it.'

24

They went outside. Alcaén glanced at her hands and saw that she didn't wear a wedding ring. He wondered what was the most direct route to this woman. He knew little about her, in fact only two things: her name was Laura Salinas and she was the woman of his dreams.

'I assume Señor Valente has already told you there's another family interested in this house.'

'Señor Valente?' said the false Alcaén, astute as ever, and preparing the way for his next strike.

'My colleague who showed you round the first time. Remember him? Dark hair, in his forties . . .'

'Oh, you mean there's someone else apart from you on this planet?' that camouflaged Alcaén should have said then, lighting up another cigarillo. However, the woman's eyes frightened him; he felt intimidated by that feline gaze, exposed to the power of her tigerish cheek-bones, her pale skin and dark-cherry lips, which he wanted to kiss to distraction, to kiss night and day, in spring and summer, in cafés and churches, inside a burning castle besieged by Tartar hordes.

'Yeah, I think I remember him: a dark-haired guy, the sort that's easy to forget.'

The girl laughed again.

'That's him. The description's spot on.'

'With you, on the other hand . . . Well, I'm completely sure . . .' Alcaén was a pair of wrestlers locked in combat; one struggling to come up with something witty, the other unwilling to overstep the mark; one opting for being careful, the other for being reckless. But both could see that the girl was getting away, vanishing irretrievably before their very eyes, a little more with each passing second, as if she were a woman of sand. '. . . that you I won't forget.'

Laura gave a weak smile and looked down at the floor. Had she blushed? For a few seconds she seemed lost for words; Alcaén sensed her efforts to disguise her embarrassment, to ensure that, when she looked up again, her eyes would have a neutral, impermeable expression.

'Thank you, you're . . . that's kind of you. Now then, unless there's anything else, I think all that remains is for you to think it over and let us have your decision. Bear in mind it's a great opportunity and there's another family that . . .'

'Look,' interrupted Alcaén, emboldened by his own daring, 'I happen to have a number of matters to attend to this morning. And as for taking a decision, I'll probably need a little more time.'

'Of course; as much as you like.'

'I'm still undecided, but I very much like this house. That said, the garage does only take two cars . . . Perhaps we could arrange another visit.'

'Certainly,' she said. Alcaén thought he detected a nuance in her voice, though he couldn't have said what it was. 'What about, say, Thursday morning?'

'The morning's out. Middle of the day, perhaps? Are you free between two and four?'

'Well, that's lunchtime. Usually I . . .'

'In that case you could show me round at two and have lunch with me afterwards.'

The girl fixed her eyes on the ground again and blushed; she said no, then she said yes:

'All right. No harm in a business lunch, is there? I shall see you on Thursday, at two o'clock.'

And that was the end of round one.

Alcaén couldn't believe that he had managed it and, on the way home, felt all that a man can feel in relation to just one thing: an immense joy and a vast emptiness; he felt happy and scared, large and small, weak and invincible. He started to plan Thursday's lunch. He imagined an expensive restaurant, an exotic menu, dazzling conversation; lingering at the table until dusk, until that moment when final precautions between two strangers give way and a new friendship begins to take hold, forming unbreakable bonds. Maybe they would have dinner together that very evening. If so, he thought to himself, he'd need some new clothes; and he might also rent a decent car. Was all that within his means? Perhaps not, but what did it matter? Love could reverse everything, it had the power to turn ruins into palaces, ashes into wood.

When the bus reached the city, he saw several beautiful women who were now only modest versions of Laura Salinas, looking upon them with the condescending gaze of the explorers of old for whom the Guadalquivir was a pale copy of the Amazon, the Ebro but a mere echo of the Nile.

He also pondered the matter of the house, telling himself that that building and Laura Salinas were somehow linked, that either he would have them both or he would have neither. Was that true? Leave aside whether it was or not – at the moment it makes no difference to us; all that matters is that Alcaén more or less saw things like this: she deserves someone better than me, so I'll have to become someone else. How was he going to become that someone else? That he didn't know yet, but he shuddered when he realised that his next thought was about the safe at his insurance company, for the money it contained and which he counted in a small office at the end of each working day. Sometimes there was a large sum, more than enough to buy whatever his heart desired. And the money was always there, unattended, all night long, until the security guards collected it first thing in the morning. It was there, divided into wads of one hundred thousands and fifty thousands, each one consisting of blue, grey, red and green banknotes. Alcaén knew everything there was to know about them: they were smooth to the touch, hypnotic; hold them in your hand and they'll produce a feeling of well-being, almost dreaminess, like when the warmth of sunshine passes through the skin and combines with the blood, engendering a sensation of other-worldly peace. At times though, as you reach for them, they cut you like a knife.

5

The Pigeon Killer

The man who never appeared in his own dreams had just killed a pigeon, but Iker Orbáiz still didn't know exactly why; so he started to wander about the room, a confused look on his face, anxiously twiddling a pen with his fingers. He'd been sure it was an ideal occupation for the character in his story ever since he found out from a newspaper that such a job existed; that the city council had cages to trap pigeons set up around the city, and employed a number of technicians to conduct tests on the birds and put down by lethal injection any found to be diseased. The discovery had excited Iker, for it seemed to him an occupation that was both clinical and morbid, completely in keeping with the life he intended to give his character. However, not knowing much more about the subject, he made a couple of phone calls and went to see what it was all about for himself.

It was a cold, cloudless day – the sort that makes people appear more fragile and the sky more clear. Iker did his best to memorise that atmosphere, which would perhaps set the tone for his story: the biting cold, the tense air, the light that appeared not so much to illuminate the surroundings as to be an entity in itself. He noted too the ill-tempered gait of passers-by, their half-white half-pink faces, their dirty boots and tobacco-coloured raincoats.

He began to assemble the words needed to explain all this.

He took a taxi, and, minutes later, was at one of the places where the pigeons were caught. It was a national medical service out-patients' clinic, one of those grey state-owned buildings that fill your heart with cement the moment you set eyes on them; the cage had been set up on the roof. The secretary he'd spoken to on the phone had given him a choice of this site or two others: the roof of the Veterinary Faculty or that of the Observatory. He'd opted for the clinic because it was the site that inspired the greatest sense of neglect, on account of its squalid atmosphere, its waiting rooms full of men and women who waited their turn with a rather melodramatic resignation and calm; its bad oxygen, laden with the smell of illness and medication.

He went over to the information booth. Inside was a woman whose surly aspect combined all the ingredients of her type: around fifty years old, hair dyed lemon-blonde, pompous manner, skin of a crunchy texture with enough lipstick to paint the front of a ministry building.

'Excuse me . . .' said Iker. 'Could you help me?'

She raised her eyes stiffly from whatever it was she was watching on the other side of the counter. She was about to lose patience. 'Good morning!' she said.

'Yes, of course, good morning. Sorry. Could you tell me how I can get to the roof?'

'Naturally, enough said. Have you brought sun-block and towel – or would you like to borrow one of ours?'

'Look – I have an appointment.'

'On the roof? Who are you – the chimney sweep?'

'You must be Mary Poppins. Don't know how I missed it. Children must adore you, I'll bet anything.'

She observed him with as much contempt as can fit onto a single face. Her eyes threw sparks. Iker decided that her weekends must be interminable and solitary; that she spent them eating tinned food and poisoning her neighbours' cats.

'Access to the roof is prohibited. You need official authorisation. I'll bet two months' salary that you don't have it.'

'I've spoken to the Environmental Officer at the council. Doctor Elían Roma is expecting me. Couldn't you call and verify it? I'll hold the earpiece so you don't strain yourself.'

'Environmental? Is this something to do with those blasted creatures?'

'That's right. They're called pigeons; lovers like walking among them in town squares. Don't tell me that's not what you do every evening.'

The receptionist gave him another choleric look. She was a true charmer: she'd have crossed the street to avoid greeting her own mother. However, she lost the will to fight when she knew what Iker was after; the matter was out of her jurisdiction, in international waters.

'Go to the lifts on the other side of reception, take one up to the tenth floor, turn right and look for a red door. Think you can manage or shall I draw you a map?'

'I think I can manage, if I keep my wits about me. Many thanks, you're most kind. What are your plans for today, after work?'

31

'Steering clear of wise guys.'

'Shame. I thought you'd probably fancy dinner with me. You know: you, me, and a pair of scented candles.'

'Really? Look, I think it's still a bit soon for that. Come back when both of us are adults and I'll see.'

Iker let her have the last word. Why not? She was a bitter, harmless creature, fighting with unusual ferocity in a very small war; someone from whom life had probably been taking, one by one, each of the things she had hoped for, without anyone trying to prevent it. Who had ever offered to help? Who had come to rescue her from her damp, dark well? Iker forgot her for ever as soon as he stepped out of the lift and started along the corridor towards the red door that led up to the roof of the clinic. Once there, he found himself in a sort of lunar landscape of antennas, skylights, water tanks. There were various chimneys, the largest of which, he saw, spewed forth a thick, immaculately white smoke, perhaps from the heating system – or perhaps something else. What needed to be burnt in a hospital? The sight of that phantasmagorical, surgical vapour rising into the air caused him to shudder.

The cage with the pigeons stood in one of the corners, five or six metres away from the cornice. Doctor Elián Roma, dressed head to toe in a rust-grey protection suit, appeared the ideal complement to the galactic moonscape. As Iker headed towards to him, he registered the sour stench coming from the birds, as well as the deafening flapping of their wings; the sinister images that metallic, effervescent sound conjured up: hearses, funeral wreaths, cemeteries. He opened his notebook and wrote all this down.

He walked up to the vet and, raising his voice, explained he needed a few facts for a book he was writing. Elián Roma looked at him in bewilderment and, for a few seconds, said nothing. Iker thought of the greedy silences that informers in detective novels keep up until the private eye hands over twenty or thirty dollars. When Elián Roma did speak, however, there was neither avarice nor usury in his voice, merely indifference. An icy, impregnable indifference, fenced round by barbed wire.

'Facts about pigeons? What sort of facts?'

'I've read, for example, that you kill some of the pigeons you catch.'

The man glanced suspiciously at the notebook on which Iker was about to write down his answers. He removed his protective visor, took off his gloves.

'Yes, that's right. We give a lethal injection to any that are too old or unhealthy. Others we put down in batches, with carbon dioxide.'

'What do you use for that? A gas chamber?'

'More or less.'

'What disease do they usually have?'

The man lit a cigarette, and looked over at the trapped birds.

'Well, at first it's only a germ called *Chlamydia psittaci*. But if not stopped in time, it becomes something more serious that's harmful to humans.'

'People can become infected?'

'They certainly can. It provokes a kind of pneumonia.'

'Aren't you afraid of catching it?'

'That's unlikely to happen so long as I wear one of these suits. Besides, if something goes wrong, I can always get vaccinated. It's a disgusting job but it's safe.'

Iker Orbáiz smiled at him, delighted by that cynical detail.

'One more question, the last one. What happens to the pigeons that get caught and turn out to have nothing? Do you set them free again?'

'We do, but not here. Some are taken to other provinces and released in forests or off a cliff. The others we put on a truck that takes them out to one of the parks beyond the city limits. It's no use, though: most find their way back into the centre.'

'And that's not good?'

The man let out a noisy laugh.

'Not good? Shall I tell you something? They're not welcome here. People hate them, except for a few tourists and the handful of nutcases who feed them every morning, give them names and feel proud when they get them to take the birdseed from their hands. Everyone else detests them. These pests ruin rooftops, stain statues, monuments, cars and washing lines. Like I said: no one wants them.'

Iker Orbáiz thanked Elián Roma and left, satisfied and excited by what he had seen and heard.

He took another taxi to the south part of the city, to visit a furniture shop that was linked to a crime: the husband of the owner had been murdered. Iker often did this – visiting the scene where an incident had just occurred, attempting to discover in the people and objects any trace of the recent drama; soaking up the macabre scent that seemed to linger in those banal places rendered singular by tragedy. Whenever asked about this habit of his, he would reply that it was fieldwork, a fact-finding mission. He may have been right: if you don't go out to collect wood, you can't make a fire.

On the way there, it occurred to him that the story about the man who never appeared in his own dreams was deserving of more than a short story, that it might make a good novel. That was exactly what Ángel Biedma had told him two nights before, en route to the Sívori. And he had said something else as well:

'Know what I would do if I were you? I'd pick someone on which to model the main character, someone I had close enough to hand to be able to study in depth, to note his every expression, his every gesture, the way he talks or moves a muscle. It strikes me that Alcaén would be a great choice. What do you think? I even like the name; you could put it in the title, No one dreams of Alcaén Sánchez, or something like that.'

For some reason, inside Iker Orbáiz that idea had grown steadily; it was on his mind throughout the day, during his inspection of the crime scene and afterwards, as he sipped a Martini in a bar; or when browsing through recent publications in two or three bookshops, or had miso soup and sushi in a Japanese restaurant, or when he bought food in a supermarket for that evening's supper. And it was still there many hours later, when finally he set off on his journey home. The moment he decided that he would do it and take Alcaén as his starting point, Iker was on a bus, and he realised suddenly how much the sky had changed since that morning: now it was violet and looked shattered, broken-up, like lilacs trampled by heedless feet.

6

Easy Money

Everyone was asleep, his family on the top floor and the guests in the bedroom downstairs, when Alcaén crept in to steal the money. Many years had passed since then, yet he remembered every second of that episode: it was a weekend and the Casares – or the Esprius, the Laforets, the Celayas, what did it matter – had arrived late at night. He recalled with absolute clarity the moment they rang at the door and he had hung up their coats in the hallway cupboard; the moment the man had taken his wallet out to show something to the others – an ID card, a photograph, a receipt – and he had seen the conspicuous bulge of notes; how afterwards, in the dark, everything – a rusty spring mattress, a dripping tap – took on a sense of menace as he felt his way down the stairs; and finally, he recalled the terrible silence as he escaped from the guest room clutching his spoils, that silence which filled him with a sense of immensity and danger, like the feeling you get when you listen to the sound of the waves from the top of a cliff.

Or perhaps not. Perhaps none of this ever happened and Alcaén Sánchez had never stolen money from guests as they lay sleeping in his parents' house. But there must have been in his past – for there is in everyone's – some slip equivalent to this, some lapse that let him feel the weight of a crime, the guilty man's inescapable anguish: it may only have been a kid's petty racket involving three or four friends; or an unsuccessful attempt to steal from a department store; or a few coins taken from a handbag. But such a thing did undoubtedly occur, and now it was back, intact, gnawing ferociously away at the heart of the Alcaén of twenty-five years later, the one who had thought about stealing from his insurance company.

But was he really going to do that? Again, it seemed to him an act of madness, suicide. For a start, a perfect crime was impossible; there always remained some loose end, a trace, that would, sooner or later, directly or indi-rectly, lead back to the culprit. He clearly remembered a conversation Iker Orbáiz and Ángel Biedma had had about fingerprints: fingerprints have four features – the arch, the ridge, the island, and the bifurcations; there are two ways to analyse them, the Henry system and the Battley system; fingerprints come in seven different types, plain arch and tented arch, accidental, loop, plain whorl, central pocket loop and double loop.

He stared at his fingertips. He felt a little dizzy. The Law is powerful, he thought, it has police officers, pris-ons, laboratories; scientists who get to the bottom of everything: the petrographer analyses the shapes in the earth formed by footprints or tyre tracks; mineral parti-cles are studied in the spectrography department, ultra-violet rays examine ink stains, serological testing deals with bloodstains; you have to be careful not to injure yourself because your name and address are written on each drop of that blood, they can be read through a microspectroscope; and no matter how much care you've taken, there'll always be a day when a couple of inspectors knock on your door; you thought it wouldn't happen and suddenly . . .

'Señor Sánchez? Are you feeling ill? You're very pale.'

Alcaén started at the sound of Laura Salinas' voice and looked around at his surroundings slightly wild-eyed, as if just brought out of a trance. 'You were only imagining things,' he told himself in an attempt to reassert control. 'You're in a restaurant; she went to the Ladies and now she's back. Before that, you were talking about destiny.'

'Very pale, am I? Strange, I've never felt better,' he said, giving her a meaningful stare. 'I could recite Lorca while winding my watch up with my toes.'

Laura laughed, this time without lowering her gaze or becoming embarrassed. Bathed in the sumptuous glow of happiness, her ochre-hued eyes were even more beautiful; on Alcaén they had a tonic effect, they made him feel agile, euphoric. Who says spells don't exist? You look down into the magic goblet and, all of a sudden, you see yourself with Laura Salinas or another like her; you see a house by the mountains, you see the dense forest, the untiring river, the love that has neither beginning nor end, like water.

'You're very amusing, you know that?'

'And you're wonderful.'

There was a great silence. A deep, clinging silence. Had he made her uncomfortable? Had he chosen the right moment to say that, or was it still too soon? You know the state Alcaén found himself in and how, when you're in that situation, logic doesn't matter and maintaining your balance isn't possible; you're walking on both velvet and burning coals; everything soothes you and everything hurts.

They were in a Thai restaurant, and it was their second date. Before that, they had eaten together on the occasion Alcaén had engineered on the pretext of needing to see the house again. Now, a few days later, he had invited her to dinner once more, only this time without using an excuse; and though at first the idea seemed to frighten her, she had eventually agreed.

On neither occasion was Laura Salinas very talkative; in fact, she showed herself continually to be an exceptionally shy person who blushed easily and became all self-conscious whenever he made a seductive move or employed a phrase with double meaning. But not only was that behaviour enough to conquer him from East to West, North to South, it achieved his unconditional surrender: Alcaén adored her, he was driven wild by her skin, her hands, her short chestnut hair, as well as the aura of rectitude and decency in which all this was wrapped.

Yet he also remembered that he had become involved with her by means of a lie, and that that lie remained there, part of every step they took. 'What will happen,' he asked himself a thousand times, obsessed by the possible consequences of his own self-created predicament, 'if she finds out I am not the man she thinks I am? What will happen when I can't buy the house or keep up this cycle of fancy restaurants and exotic food?' There was only one thing that separated him from her, he concluded: money. How could he get some? He told himself that he knew of no honourable way; that in this perverse, twisted world there is no short cut that leads the poor upwards; but there is a direct link between dirty deeds and easy money. He also knew that the idea of stealing it was ridiculous, unbearable, though not as unbearable as living without Laura – that he couldn't even consider. How without Laura? Why without Laura? Certain things are like that, hard to imagine without the object for which they are intended: a neon sign unlit, a window with no glass, an empty coffin.

That night after they left the restaurant, Alcaén accompanied her to a taxi rank. On the way they spoke very little. He felt great anxiety, a strong desire to put his arms around her. He controlled himself; but when he saw they were nearing the car in which she was going to leave, when he saw its green light and the driver removing the For Hire card from inside the windscreen, he took hold of her hand and whispered:

'I hope I didn't upset you earlier . . . when I spoke the truth.'

She lowered her eyes again. She seemed uncomfortable, but not angry.

'You didn't upset me,' Laura replied, acknowledging the intimacy in his words. 'I thought it was . . . well . . .'

'Yes?'

'Sweet,' she said, freeing her hand. 'Very sweet of you.'

He, at that point, wanted to kiss her; would have wanted that more than anything else in the world. But she did nothing, made no move at all to allow him the path to her lips. The taxi driver started the engine.

'Listen . . .' said Alcaén Sánchez too late and by now to himself, right after Laura had gone. '. . . Earlier you asked me if I believed in predestination. I do believe in it. I think all I've done in my life so far is to slowly get nearer and nearer to you; I've been walking towards you ever since I was born.'

He made his way home through deserted streets and half-lit districts, his hands in his pockets and his mind dispirited by dark thoughts. He was in trouble, caught in his own trap, like all liars. He was at that crossroads where to tell the truth could be as damaging as to go on pretending. And what if he, quite simply, told her everything? What did that everything mean, though? 'Listen, my darling: I'm an impostor, I don't have a peseta, I'm not going to be buying anything, I'm a nobody, have faith in me.' He had to make a decision, and do so soon; one that was firm and on which there was no going back, a resolution of the sort that takes us away from our own life, that can change its course, alter its meaning. He would do whatever was necessary; he would do it despite everything, come hell or high water, so that Laura would not walk away. Again he started to plot a means of stealing the money from the insurance company. It was a crazy idea. It was so unreal that it didn't even seem impossible.

We won't follow him to his apartment, because I think that part of my job is done now; that there's no need for me to provide greater detail or further clarification about either his emotional state or the extent and nature of the harm that awaited him. You know already what was the misfortune that sent Alcaén wandering pitifully around inside a stranger who was also called Alcaén Sánchez and who, in many respects, turned out to be his opposite; there's nothing more I have to explain, as I suppose most of you will have been in love at some point and, if so, you'll know in what that adversity, that raging spiritual ill, consists: you think with your heart, you suffer with your brain.

In other words, you become weak, but you also become dangerous.

7

The Man of Sand

Ángel Biedma was the first to wake up and, as was his habit, did so with voluptuous sloth, like someone rousing himself from the dense undergrowth of a narcotic. He came to life in a slow sequence of arching stretches and concave postures, enjoying that warm sensation of emergence; he felt – as he did every morning too – a lurch of sweet confusion on seeing in the other half of the bed his partner's naked body; on confirming with the tiniest of caresses its lovely defencelessness and inviting skin. 'I could kill you,' he thought. 'I could kill you now, if I wanted to.' Afterwards he went into the kitchen, put on some coffee, and prepared some toast and juice, but doing all with a meticulous economy of movement, in none of these tasks exerting himself more than was absolutely necessary and, as such, reduced to a sort of abbreviated version of himself, albeit one that was already in essence Ángel Biedma – a scrupulous, fussy man for whom order constituted the guiding principle in all things, the core from which the other major qualities derived, from efficiency to honesty, from vigour to prudence. His entire life from the outset had been calculated and organised around this axis, and he considered the results to have been very good: broadly speaking, he could think of nothing he had ever really wanted that he did not have.

And yet his relationship with Iker Orbáiz was the most precious thing he had. Why? Wasn't that boy, in more ways than one, a perturbing and illogical presence in the midst of so much order and so much discipline? In fact, though lucid, wasn't Iker also chaotic, intuitive and anarchic; in other words, the diametric opposite of Doctor Ángel Biedma? Perhaps he was. But don't let yourselves be fooled: if you add two and two together, you'll deduce that the doctor in our story – as well as being a satisfied person – was also a domineering individual who, in the end, got nowhere with his restraint and his irreproachable rules; who got nowhere with his contempt for confusion and incompetence; with his theory that an error is always the antechamber to further error of even greater magnitude. Because there was something that Iker possessed that he lacked: talent. At Iker's side, he accomplished what he had never achieved by himself, namely creating something of his own, inventing it; unearthing things that never previously existed. He brought the good sense, Iker the genius. One brought the arsenal, the other the aim. Did that not make them the perfect partners?

Ángel delighted in his role as instigator and confidant; he felt happy during the endless discussions about each story or project; he felt rewarded whenever any of his suggestions helped give one of the boy's stories its definitive form. He enjoyed his role a great deal, and he took it as seriously as everything else that concerned him – he devoted an enormous amount of energy to Iker's ideas, giving them careful thought as soon as he got up and before he fell asleep, looking for snags or solutions in spare moments between his consultations at the hospital and as he drove on his way to work.

And this is what he did for the story about the man who never appeared in his own dreams. To start with, Iker had had some very good ideas, like making the main character a vet who exterminated pigeons on the rooftops of a large city. But as the plot progressed the character started, in Ángel's opinion, to go a little cold; become more and more like cardboard, less believable. Then he came up with the ruse of copying Alcaén Sánchez's features, using him as a model. It was a good strategy – a sort of transfusion. After all, Ángel told himself, weren't they both just a couple of poor devils with a lot in common and, as such, interchangeable? Iker had all the necessary material to hand, the only thing he needed was to go there and collect it. Ángel advised him not to say anything to Alcaén; it would be more astute, he said, to coax things out of him gradually, rather than put him on his guard.

From then on, that's what they did night after night; first they robbed him of his features and gestures, then they raided his mind: they asked him about his childhood, his family, his secret likings, his personal tastes, his private habits; gradually they dispossessed him of everything and, at first, creating the main character in their story had proved to be a simple task, as easy as kicking over a sand castle and, with the remains, making another in its stead.

Alcaén, for his part, felt flattered by his friends' new attitude towards him; day after day he emptied himself for them without precaution, not really understanding what they found so special about the insignificant events of a life as normal as his, but happy to have relinquished the subordinate role he'd had at their gatherings and to unexpectedly find himself the target of their interest. He also felt slightly intimidated by the sudden attention lavished on him by Ángel Biedma, ordinarily so polite but also so reserved, so cold. Alcaén had always been sure he was not much to Ángel's liking, that for some reason Ángel looked down on him, perhaps for being a mere clerk in an office or not having a university degree; or perhaps because he had interfered in his long chats with Iker Orbáiz. Now Ángel's attitude towards him had changed; it was as different from his previous attitude as night is from morning: he looked at Alcaén encouragingly, followed extremely closely the things he related about, for example, his relationship with Laura Salinas, their meetings, which he described in minute, obsessive detail.

Ángel Biedma was eight or ten years older than either Iker and Alcaén; he must have been nearly forty, but he looked older because of the way he dressed, which on his visits to Sívori was always casual yet proper – unfailingly well-pressed trousers, occasionally daring but never loud shirts; pullovers in brown, lavender or navy blue. If Iker Orbáiz had wanted to describe him from head to foot in one of his stories, he would have noted the wide forehead, the muddy brown eyes, and the often evasive stare in which suddenly a glint might appear, striking and dull, like the sound of a gong; the nose was unremarkable, and the combination of too-thin lips with a forceful chin gave his face an expression that was bold and shrivelled in equal measure; his body, even tucked away under the discreet loose-fitting garments that softened its contours, gave hints of being robust and compact: one of those men who, undressed, turns out to be three times more muscular than you'd have imagined after seeing him with his clothes on.

But, even before starting, Iker would doubtless have known that none of this was important, that these were only secondary characteristics. For the core of Ángel Biedma was contained in his hands – abundant, biblical hands with which he underlined whatever he said; hands whose rhythm accompanied each speech and phrase, and which he used to give his words extraordinary shapes: dragon-words, starfish-words, wolf-words, spider-words . . . His personality was concentrated in those almighty hands which, at that precise moment, he was gazing at, after finishing his breakfast in the kitchen of his home: they rested on the table, one on either side of his cup of coffee, so immobile that they seemed dormant, in a sense alien to the rest of him. He was looking at them but not seeing them, for his mind was elsewhere, thinking about the man who never appeared in his own dreams and about how that text had ground to a halt. He wondered why, and deduced the obvious: Alcaén Sánchez's life was not enough; following it would not lead them sufficiently far.

He could guess how Iker must have lost heart at seeing his novel run into difficulties, at seeing it grind to a halt little by little, irremediably; fall ever more silent as the paragraphs, the sentences, the words petered out. Ángel Biedma imagined this silence to be similar to that following the coming to a standstill of a train, that violent stillness in which scratched rails, boiling steam, red-hot cables and rusted steel nuts all dissolve.

What he believed, that morning while he finished breakfast, was this: that he could decipher from a distance what was going through Iker's mind, as if the two of them were like those prisoners in films who communicate from cell to cell by tapping a lead beaker against the prison pipes. The first time they met, Ángel remembered, he had taken hold of the young man's hand and had explained to him it was a psychic hand; that according to the laws of palmistry there exist psychic hands, philosophic hands, hands that are energetic, square, elemental . . . He explained to him how the palm of a hand is divided into mounts and lines; he showed him which was the mount of Venus, that of Mars, where to find those of Saturn, Apollo, Jupiter, Mercury; he pointed out to him which was the line of the heart, which were those of the head, of fate, of health and of life; he told him that his ring of Venus showed that he was a person with talent, with a sensitivity for Art. He finished by reminding Iker of the phrase in the Bible that his mother – the person who taught him what he knew about palmistry – always used to end with whenever she talked to him about that subject: 'God placed signs in the hands of men, that all men might know their works.'

Ángel remembered all that; and afterwards started to look through a list in which he had noted down writers' names and the dates of their death. Very soon it would be eighty-nine years since the death of Tolstoy.

The last sips of his coffee tasted bitter.

8

False Blood

On the day before the robbery at the insurance company, Alcaén pulled a cable out of the small electric radiator in the room where he counted the money every afternoon. He did it just before he went out – his hands trembled, blood rushed to his face, and he had an attack of diarrhoea, despite this being the only part of his plan that was straightforward; despite only needing to disable the plug just before he went out and to then leave the door shut until the next morning. It was a tiny room adjacent to the director's office, and the procedure they followed was always the same: when there remained an hour or so before the close of business, Alcaén and the director – a man whose implacable baldness and sharp profile lent his face a numismatic severity, and whom all the employees respectfully called Señor Montero or Boss – would unlock the safe and transfer its contents into bags, which they took to a small room where, alone, Alcaén would tally up the various amounts; once the totals had been calculated and recorded in the ledgers, Alcaén would arrange the banknotes into one – sometimes two – steel-sided security cases, then call through on the internal line to Señor Montero, who would come and check his work, after which both of them would return the day's takings to the safe, until eight o'clock sharp the next morning, when this money was entrusted to the security guards. All these bureaucratic procedures were assumed to weave an impenetrable layer of protection around the company's assets, and so it would have, but for one small detail: Señor Montero never checked the steel-sided cases properly; he did not verify their contents because, after six years of working with Alcaén, his faith in him was absolute; which meant that when his subordinate notified him each afternoon that he was ready to replace the money in the safe, all the director did was to give it a brief glance and say: 'OK, Sánchez, close that up, and let's go and leave it somewhere secure, out of reach of our light-fingered friends', or something along those lines, as that was the way he talked, employing ceremonious phrases full of purely ornamental details, which gave whatever he said the semblance of a verdict or, in many cases, the solemnity of a manifesto. His pronouncement uttered, Señor Montero would lead the way out of the room, back to the safe, leaving Alcaén, unsupervised, to follow and close the locks on the cases.

And it was on that twofold lack of precaution that Alcaén's entire plan was based: he had sewn a second lining into his overcoat, with a series of pockets in which to hide the wads of banknotes and in which, beforehand, he planned to conceal several small bags of sand that was the same as the sand from the ashtrays that stood by the lifts; when he entered the room where he balanced the day's receipts and where the electric radiator wasn't working, the temperature would be low enough to justify going back to fetch his overcoat; while alone in the room,

Alcaén would scratch the locks on the cases with a screwdriver or knife and replace the money with the sand but leave a surface layer – all that Montero would see – of banknotes he intended to remove as soon as his boss's back was turned, in the fifteen, twenty seconds it always took him to seal the locks. Before all that, he'd have broken a window in a small, rarely used bathroom on the floor above and poured down the toilet almost all of the sand from the two ashtrays there, one by the door to the bathroom, the other by the lifts, making sure he left no traces. And he planned to round his strategy off with three further tricks: he had bought a pair of shoes that were two sizes too small for him; in the morning he'd pick up a cigarette butt from some place, and, the evening before, he'd have got a small sample of someone else's blood from the Sívori by leaving in the men's toilet a bar of soap in which he'd concealed several tiny pieces of a razor blade; no doubt someone washing their hands would cut themselves on it and leave behind a trace of blood on the white porcelain surface of the washbasin. Alcaén intended to smear that blood onto one of the pieces of glass from the broken window at his office, and to throw the cigarette butt inside the safe when he put the money away. He'd also make sure that he left a footprint there, perhaps on the wall, and another on the outside of the window, by wetting the sole and applying it by hand.

The robbery would be discovered the next morning, at about nine-thirty or ten o'clock, as soon as the staff at the bank opened the cases. Naturally, he would be questioned by the police and considered a suspect from the outset; but the police would also find, on the butt and on the broken glass, blood and saliva that were not his. And, to further strengthen his alibi, he was certain that Señor Montero wouldn't declare not having checked either the contents or the locks of the cases – locks which Alcaén would, of course, not have closed – as this would have been to admit intolerable negligence in the eyes of the company's owners.

'The thieves came in through the window,' said a detective conjured up by Alcaén's imagination, 'and one of them cut himself on a piece of broken glass; they managed to work out the combination of the safe, stole the money from the cases – the locks show signs of having been forced – then switched the banknotes with sand, so as to buy time: that way the lack of weight wouldn't give them away in advance and the robbery wouldn't be discovered at eight-thirty at the insurance company but at the bank, almost two hours later. It's obvious they took the sand from the office ashtrays, because two of them are emptier than the others, and also that the crime was committed during the night, after the cleaners had left, because the earth was fresh. The thieves almost certainly wore gloves, as there're no fingerprints anywhere except for those of the manager and the cashier. We know one of the thieves smoked Marlboros and another, or perhaps the same one, wore size 41 shoes.'

Alcaén went over his plan dozens and dozens of times; sometimes it seemed to him infallible and at other times, as fanciful and impracticable as it probably does to you right now. Of course, it was not without its inspired parts

– the razor blade in the bar of soap, the cigarette picked up at random – but it was also full of risks. Risks which receded and dwindled when he thought of Laura, as soon as he assembled all her aspects in his mind: the chestnut hair, the ochre eyes, the delicate skin, her aura of honesty, and all the other things which in his eyes rendered her almost unreal, less a person than a symbol, a sort of mythological being more related to sirens and tritons than to ordinary people; more readily linked with legends about centaurs and unicorns than with the unemployment rate or the electricity bill. What was he going to offer Laura Salinas – he wondered for the last time on the eve of his heist, right before leaving his apartment to go to the Sívori – if he didn't bring off the robbery? His sixty-square-metre life, his two hundred thousand pesetas a month, and one half of his chest of drawers? He had to have the money, and he had to buy the house: you can't keep a unicorn in a cowshed.

That was why he was going to go through with it the next day. That was why he had pulled the cable out of the radiator in his office that afternoon. And that trivial act, that first step of his plan, made him feel it was no longer possible to oppose his destiny, that the madness was already under way.

He broke the razor blade up with a pair of pliers, and inserted three or four fragments into the soap. Then he left his apartment, and, while he walked towards the Sívori, he began to observe certain individuals smoking in their cars, or in the street or at bus stops; feeling all the while a morbid sensation as he selected his candidate, feeling the sense of power of those who exercise some form of authority over others. Finally, his hands protected by gloves, he picked up the cigarette butt he'd just seen thrown down at the entrance to a bar by a man of about his size – a man who would certainly have fitted through the broken window of the toilet at his office. He wondered who that man was, what his profession was, whether he was married, how close the police spectrographs and microspectroscopes would manage to get to him, what type of fingerprints he had, if they were plain arch or tented arch, if they were accidental or central pocket loop. Part of the man's life was inscribed on that cigarette, Alcaén assumed: his sex, his DNA, his bone structure; even his age, what illnesses he had had, what he ate on the night of the crime.

Who was to say that his plan wasn't perfect, after all? For how would they ever work out that the sum of his traps equalled zero? At the end of the day, the world was full of unsolved crimes and unpunished criminals. What if, though, for whatever reason, he didn't manage to fool them? What if he made a mistake, his nerves let him down? He thought again about Laura Salinas, about kissing her lips and exploring her skin, deciphering her incalculable body. And what if something unexpected happened? What if instead of putting him in the clear, one of his ploys pointed straight to him? He stopped tormenting himself as he reached the Sívori. That evening and the next he needed to proceed with care, to do and say only those things which he wanted others to remember that he had said and done, in case they were questioned.

He waved across the room at Ángel Biedma, who was already waiting for him, and went to leave the bar of soap in the toilets. It was only a preliminary move, hardly a compromising act as yet; but Alcaén was already very afraid, he felt a murky, pounding fear, the same trembling in his legs and the same spasms in his stomach of a few hours earlier, when he had pulled the cable out of the radiator. It was a damaging, insoluble fear, yet he tried tenaciously to resist it, he made frantic efforts to wipe it from his face, like a man bailing out a boat with a bucket. However, when he saw his reflection in the mirror he looked so different that he gave himself several unceremonious slaps to restore calm to those quivering features; to bring the colour back to that gaunt countenance, which, in the brash light of the bathroom, had taken on an almost spectral appearance. The slaps did little to put matters right.

Perhaps he would feel better very soon, when he went back to the toilet to collect the false robber's blood.

9

An Empty Mine Full of Gold

'That morning, at about eleven o'clock, Alcaén Sánchez walked into a supermarket,' Iker Orbáiz read.

He was on his way back from murdering pigeons in the gas chamber, and was experiencing his usual reaction: inside him the dead birds continued to flutter, he could still hear their cooing, the funereal sound of their wings, the explosion of noise when he released the carbon monoxide and the creatures sensed their end; in his hands he could still feel the bodies of the birds he killed by lethal injection, their momentary stillness as he jabbed the needle in, how for the next fifteen, twenty seconds they would struggle, and then suddenly crumple, take on that unusable look that lifeless things have.

'That unusable look,' said Iker aloud, 'or perhaps dislocated would be better. That dislocated look.'

He said a hello to the two security guards at the entrance, and was met with a neutral, deliberately opaque look from them that meant: don't bother ingratiating yourself with us, we're paid to kick your arse, not to say good morning. They were two surly, sour-faced types, identical to the rest of their profession and species; with military-seeming heads into which were compacted the tortoise eyes of a Robert Mitchum, an imperious nose, despotic cheekbones, lips forever twisted into a bitter expression, and chins that seemed the work of a Nazi chisel. They wore bottle-green uniforms, and their movements had about them a ponderous arrogance. They had packed shoulders and violent necks, thoraxes the size of kitchen tables, and the kind of hard, impassive hands that fit a bloodstained monkey wrench. Disgust showing on their faces, they talked without looking at one another, their gazes locked onto any customer who might be suspicious. Their conversations must have been as agile as JCBs ploughing through an obstacle course.

Alcaén wondered if even those two men appeared in their dreams from time to time. And he wondered the same about all the other people who at that moment were moving about inside the store, pushing trolleys full of meat and fish, of vegetables and bottles, sausages, desserts, videotapes, detergents . . . He saw a woman cross something out in a notebook, and another who was dressed in a mustard-coloured suit. He saw a man staring at his watch. He wondered if it was any one of them who, the next morning, was going to be dead.

For a while he pretended to be browsing the shelves, making sure the security guards weren't after him, and thinking about a house for sale he'd just visited outside the city – a small house with a garden which like so many others he'd seen on his days off he

*could never afford on his vet's salary, but one which,
like these others, had given him the sporadic pleasure
of impersonating a future owner, the satisfaction of
taking his place for an hour, as he had looked out over
its balconies, opened its wardrobes, or wandered
through its garden, among blue hammocks and
thought-inviting trees. He liked to leave behind brief
fragments of his life in these houses, some of which,
on occasion, he remembered as if they had really once
been his.*

*Next he thought again of Laura Salinas, the woman
he was in love with and who was beyond his reach,
because she was too good for him or he too mediocre
for a woman of her sort. Didn't that come to the same
thing? He supported that thought with something his
father had said to him once: all defeats are the same,
indistinguishable; unlike victories, they can't be
ranked from best to worse. Maybe that was true. He
remembered his father; in four or five flashes, he
remembered their life together – he saw his father taking him to school every morning, listening to football
matches on a transistor radio, wearing a dark-grey
fire-resistant overcoat, eating in silence at the head of
the table; he saw him become uncontrollably
depressed when he became a widower, shutting himself up in his bedroom night after night, tapping end-
lessly away on an ancient typewriter, without anyone
knowing why or what for until six months later, when
he departed this life, and in a locked drawer they discovered sheets and sheets of paper filled with names,*

hundreds of names of people, each one followed by a number: Manuela García Puigcerdá, 85; José Francisco Azpeitia Ferrer, 79; Carlos Riquelme Urdiales, 62 . . . That was what he had been copying out for months – the list of the deceased from the newspapers. How could you then not ask yourself once again – and perhaps once and for all – the same unanswerable questions: Why? What for?

Alcaén spent a few more moments wandering along the supermarket aisles before, finally, he went over to the fruit section, waited until he was alone, and picked up an apple. He glanced around and, when he was sure he wasn't observed, he injected the apple with a lethal dose of the poison used to kill the pigeons, before putting it back among the others.

Afterwards he bought several cartons of milk and some yoghurts, and made his way towards the bus stop, thinking about the woman in the mustard-coloured dress, about the man who'd been staring at his watch, standing by a pyramid of jars of coffee.

Iker re-read these pages of his novel carefully, crossing out some words, replacing them with others, and then putting back some of those he had crossed out; but he could not make the slightest headway with the story. He cast an anxious look at the typewritten pages, and was struck by the despairing certainty that it was in fact nothing more than stagnant water. He got up to light a cigarette and paced furiously about the room. What was it that he had? A good story but one that still lacked something, he told himself. A large, ill-defined some-

61

thing. He told himself, too, that he was probably not capable of writing that novel or any other. Or perhaps he just needed to keep on searching, to dig deeper and deeper into his character's depths. Or perhaps Ángel Biedma was right, and what his work lacked was some action, some trigger, some extraordinary occurrence. But of what kind? What sort of action could you attribute to a man of Alcaén Sánchez's temperament without it seeming unbelievable? Where to look for it – from what unseen angle?

He put on some clothes and left his apartment. It was an unpleasant night, with damp side streets that smelled of phosphorus, and an inclement sky into which rose columns of smoke from the central heating systems. It was the same night that Dostoevsky had died on, in St Petersburg, 108 years ago. He began making notes, but shortly afterwards he stopped. What was the point? He'd go for a walk around the neighbourhood, and then on to the Sívori for an involved and futile conversation with Ángel Biedma trying to find something inside Alcaén Sánchez.

What was this something? Iker Orbáiz did not know that yet, obviously. As a matter of fact, neither he nor Ángel knew anything at all. Their situation was this: they had struck a seam of gold, and thought it was empty.

10

Saturn Devouring his Children

'A false advertisement?' Alcaén Sánchez asked. 'I'm not quite sure what you mean by that.'

Ángel Biedma looked at him suspiciously. They were in the Sívori, and Alcaén had just been telling him, for the thousandth time, about his visits to houses that were for sale, about the pleasure it gave him to explore every inch of these luxury homes he could never afford – homes which were a world away from him but which, nevertheless, were his while he walked about inside them; for a few moments they belonged to him as he entered their bedrooms, as he strode over their fine-wood floors, as he sat down on their porches to enjoy a foretaste of long winter evenings with their smell of wood fires or mild July nights broken only by the deafening, beautiful sound of the dogs barking.

'Very simple, really. It's an experiment I've thought of to stimulate Iker, to help him with something he's writing; what you have to do is call up one or two newspapers and tell them you want to place an advertisement.'

'An advertisement for a house.'

'That's right.'

'But for a house that doesn't exist.'

'Exactly. When the people interested turn up at the address you've given, they'll find a vacant plot of land or an empty ruin. It'd be a way of getting revenge.'

'Getting revenge? Who am I supposed to want to get revenge on, and for what?'

'How should I know? For your bad luck,' Ángel answered, his tone somewhat bad-tempered. 'For your lack of opportunities. For everything in general and nothing in particular.'

'But I'd never behave like that. Why should I?'

'You might not, but some people would. Iker's character is one such person.'

'But why? What would they have to gain?'

'I don't think they have any particular reason, it's more a case of a need, an impulse. And in any case, I don't care, I don't want to know why they do it, but what it feels like. That's what I'm asking – for you to do it and explain it to us. Do you understand? I'm asking you to pose for Iker as though he were a painter and you were his model. That's all. Forget about what you would or wouldn't do. He's Goya and he tells you to be Saturn, you can't turn round and tell him: "But master, I would never eat my own child!"'

Alcaén pretended a great deal of that baffling explanation had gone over his head, because that was the way he acted in Iker and Ángel's company – making out that he was a bit slower than he actually was with the same skill that, in the presence of Laura, he made out he was twice as clever. Why did he do that? I don't suppose there was a real reason; it was merely part of his character. And don't start telling me you find that confusing. Would any of you know the reason for each one of your actions? The characters of nearly all novels are perfect, systematic, they never go from a to c without first passing by way of b, they know how to explore their own minds, they know exactly how much of themselves to give away, they know when to let go of one liana to catch hold of the next. If your lives too are like that, then my name's Frank Sinatra and I was once married to Ava Gardner. No; there's no way your lives could be like that because, the truth is, you're confused and illogical; you're coherent at 12 a.m. and crazy at 1 p.m., you're as brave and as frightened as everyone else. Shall I tell you that you can be just as petty or sublime as circumstances dictate, just as heartless or merciful, just as cruel or compassionate? I know these things, remember that. Don't forget I've fallen low enough to know all about you, to know that any one of us is exactly the same as everyone else. Equally clean, and equally dirty. And now, if you'll stop interrupting me, I'd like to go on with the story.

'What I'm asking you is quite straightforward,' Ángel continued. 'It's a question of Iker being able to write about some of the things that have happened to you, only in reverse.'

'In reverse?'

'In a different order: first I invent what happened to you, then you do it,' Dr Biedma said, in his monotonous, equable voice, so characteristic of those of his profession, confessors and bad lawyers.

'All right, I'll do it. I don't understand it, but I'll do whatever you want.'

He got up to go to the bathroom. He had just seen, at the bar, talking to Gloria, a customer who kept waving his arms about and was kicking up a great fuss. The man was fifty or thereabouts, of average height and about 180 pounds; clean-shaven, with dark hair turning silver at the temples. He was wearing black Terylene trousers, a polo-neck jumper and an ash-coloured overcoat. Although actually none of these details held much importance for Alcaén. All that mattered to him was that the man's hands were bloodstained.

By the time he returned to the table, Iker Orbáiz had arrived, and the first thing he said was:

'Alcaén, can I ask you a question? I hope you don't mind. It's for something I'm writing. Are your parents still alive or dead?'

'They're both alive, thank God. My mother is called Dolores, and is a diabetic. My father's called Nicolás, and owns a jewellery shop. I don't know if that's of any use to you.'

Iker let out a sigh, and stared at him sadly.

'No, I don't think that's of any use at all.'

11

A Storm Begins

The sunlight was offensive; it threw salt in his eyes, swollen from worry and lack of sleep, filling them with acid tears creating a shifting film of underwater objects: a letterbox, a lamp post, a public statue. That night he had been unable to sleep. He had spent it awake and in the dark in the living room of his apartment, tormenting himself with hypothetical oversights or flaws in his plan to rob the insurance company; prey to an acute sense of isolation, as if that tiny space in which he found himself were part of a house that was ten times larger, an enormous house in which the rest of the rooms were empty.

At times he would stare at his reflection in the mirror for fifteen or twenty seconds, until he turned himself into a stranger, into someone to whom to attribute that unrecognisable face transfigured by exhaustion and panic. At other times, he took down the overcoat to check that the double lining could take the weight of the bags of sand, that the seams of the pockets would hold firm; he made certain he knew exactly how to handle the shoe with which he was going to leave the footstep by the broken window, the small bottle with the blood from the man who'd cut himself in the Sívori, the screwdriver to scratch the locks on the cases, the cigarette he'd picked up in the street.

At half past ten he had telephoned Laura Salinas to ask if that Sunday she'd again like to go to the races – the place he had taken her the last time they went out together. Laura, in that polite way of hers and without yet giving him a clear answer, admitted she had enjoyed herself on that occasion, that she liked all the yelling of the people who'd placed bets, the rusty smell of the horses, the scent of the wet earth. Then, with an abrupt change of subject, she asked if that Saturday he was going to the agency to put down the deposit on the house. Alcaén told her that he would.

'Of course. I'll go to your office. And, if you were in Hell itself, I'd go to Hell.'

'Thanks.'

'I mean that.'

'Yes. Maybe you do.'

'Laura . . . Listen . . . Laura?'

'I'm listening.'

'I really want to see you.'

There was a moment of silence.

'OK,' she said, and hung up.

Alcaén recalled the night at the racecourse, how that infinitely restrained and formal woman had let herself go for a few moments while they watched the races; how she held on to his arm as they went down to the edge of the track to see the finishes; cheered on her jockey and shouted the names of the thoroughbreds at the top of her voice: 'Come on, Adelantado, come on, come on, yes, yes, come on!' Or: 'Run, Perdido, go, go, go, go!' Alcaén paid for all the bets with the generosity of a man accustomed to casinos, to expensive fountain pens and gold cigarette lighters; telling her each time that it was his treat, and he paid the restaurant bill too. When the moment came to say good night, Laura gave him a quick kiss on the lips. A very light, barely perceptible kiss, but one that caused him an immense, catastrophic burn; a fire that ravaged entire acres of Alcaén Sánchez.

In any case, that morning, as sunlight stung his eyes and fear tensed his muscles, he tried to forget all this in order to concentrate on the task at hand. In his pockets he could feel the weight of the two bags of sand he'd collected, fistful by fistful, over the course of a couple of weeks, from the office ashtrays.

He worked throughout the day as though on autopilot, without paying any great attention to the papers he filled in or to the people explaining their accidents, their fractures, the flaws in the engines or bodywork of their cars. He simply took no notice of them, except to silently hate them.

During the lunch hour he was very careful to appear his usual self, even if he wasn't; he tried to talk about trivial matters and to be no more unsociable or nicer, no more witty or more taciturn than normal. After coffee, he watched the last part of the television news in the bar, along with his other colleagues, and discussed the sports news. Nothing about his behaviour was different, or drew attention to itself. It was just a normal afternoon and the same old Alcaén Sánchez.

At 5 p.m. he went to make some photocopies; he went up to the toilet on the second floor, put on a pair of latex gloves, carefully broke the window pane and tipped some

69

blood onto the edge of several of the shards; then he unfolded the sole from the shoe two sizes too small for him that he'd cut out the day before and carried folded up in a pocket of his jacket and, wetting it first with some water, he printed a footstep onto the outside wall of the building. All this took him less than five minutes.

Back at his desk once more, he spent the time filing and entering information into the computer. He also made a telephone call to the small ads section of the newspaper; using the words Ángel Biedma had suggested, he gave his personal details and the supposed address of the property, and dictated the text: 'House, four bedrooms, very spacious living room, dining room, fitted kitchen, two en-suite bathrooms, attic, double garage, $1,000m^2$ land'. He felt nothing in particular as he did so.

At 5.20 p.m., he called Señor Montero on the internal line. His secretary picked up the phone. Her name was Virginia, she wore red nail varnish, and in the world there must have been half a dozen things more unpleasant than her voice, including leprosy and losing both arms in battle, but no more than that.

'Director's office, hellllloooooo? You're through to Virginia Urquijo.'

'Virginia, it's Alcaén. Is the boss free?'

'Not for you. For you he's busy . . . Just joking. Don't get angry with me now, eh? Putting you through.'

Were you, perhaps, surprised by this passage, this short grotesque interval? Would you say it ruins the tension, breaks up the rhythm of the story? The same thought occurred to Alcaén. So much so, that that routine, childish incident upset him more than anything else that day; it was enough to unleash all his demons, and I'm sure you'll understand why: he had spent hours being lethargic, feeling on the margins of everything, hidden under a bell jar; hours feeling immune to reality – and safe from it too. But in the face of the avalanche created by that silly woman, her foolish jokes and shrill screeching voice, his hands began to tremble again and his stomach to churn, because all that was the prelude to the robbery – the old, honourable Alcaén Sánchez's last sight of land. Next to appear after Virginia Urquijo would be Señor Montero, and then Alcaén was going to shut himself away in an office with the day's takings. Was all this really happening to him?

As he watched the avalanche near, as he sensed the imminent danger, his fears and doubts returned one by one. Wouldn't they be suspicious of the trick overcoat? Wouldn't some of the sand leak out? And what if, today of all days, the director decided to check the cases? He thought about the broken window in the office toilet, about the blood added to the shards of glass and about the man from whom he'd taken it. Who was he? Where was he at this very moment? Alcaén gripped the receiver tighter, thinking about his family and about himself as well: his mother put some water on to boil and broke open an ampoule of insulin; his father bent over a wedding ring in the back room of his jewellery shop; twenty-five years earlier Alcaén got on a bicycle.

'Montero speaking!' said the director suddenly, on the other end of the line. There was no reply. 'Hello? Are you there, Sánchez? Can you hear me?'

Alcaén slipped his hand into the pocket of his overcoat and felt the screwdriver he had ready. Then, for an instant, he closed his eyes. In the streets outside, it seemed to him a storm was breaking. He thought he could hear the rain chewing away at the city with its lead teeth.

'Yes, Señor Montero, I'm here,' he said. And, after a few brief words, he began to make his way towards the insurance company's safe.

12

You'll Never Forget Ramona Durango

Ángel Biedma woke in the middle of the night. He'd had a nightmare of which he remembered little, barely a handful of unrelated images – a tower, a woman in a red skirt, a swamp – but he knew that he had been running, because his forehead was covered in sweat and his heart was racing furiously. Or perhaps he hadn't been running – he had been in a fight with someone, for the muscles of his arms ached, as if from a struggle. And, as always, the bones he'd broken in his legs and feet ached too. Can bones ache? His could; his had tormented him ever since he had that car accident in Barcelona; he suffered the endless torture of broken kneecaps and shattered tibias, of crushed scaphoid bones and fractured ankle-bones.

He got up and went to the kitchen for a glass of hot milk. While it warmed up on the hob, he took his wallet from the top of the refrigerator, picked out the note he intended to use in the morning to pay for the newspapers, bread and perhaps one or two pastries, held it up to the light and gave it a kiss, which was one of the many superstitions he had inherited from his mother: If you kiss them, they'll come back to you, she used to say.

'Ramona Durango,' he said, and glanced up at the ceiling, as if at the sound of her name she'd come tumbling down on him. 'If you kiss them, they'll come . . . What nonsense!'

He recalled one by one those maxims and magic formulae of his mother's, how much they used to embarrass him as a boy when he saw her do that sort of thing in public – patiently place all the coins tails up on the counter when paying for a coffee or *horchata*; or at the bank, walk up each one of the steps right foot first; at the greengrocer's, kiss thousand-peseta notes before handing them over with an air of personal loss to the girl at the till; but Ángel had to admit, too, that he had never forgotten them, that he still practised those small rites in secret and that, deep down and no matter how odd they seemed, he obeyed those absurd rules rigorously: never smell a dead flower, never take a lighted match from someone else's hand, if you spill salt throw a little over your shoulder, count to thirteen three times whenever you see a hearse, never blow a candle out with your eyes open, and a long list of other charms and omens. That had been his first thought when he regained consciousness after his traffic accident in Barcelona: What didn't I do right? What antidote for misfortune did I forget?

He shook his head, smiling to himself: what an incredible person Ramona Durango had been; how special, and also how eccentric; it was so hard for him to accept that she had died, to imagine her in the ground reduced to a mass of dust. He stood up and went to the room where she had always slept, opened several drawers that still contained her clothes, a trunk full of shoes, the wardrobe in which her dresses hung: they seemed to him objects

74

from the other side, a visible part of the beyond. 'Never touch the belongings of the dead', he told himself, then closed the door of the wardrobe.

Sometimes, when he was with Iker Orbáiz, sipping his beer in three small doses or meticulously lining his coins up on the bar in the Sívori, he felt certain Iker would notice Ángel's geometric system, that pattern of behaviour full of symmetries and consistencies, in which nothing was rash or left to chance; and he felt certain, too, that Iker wouldn't like it. But the boy had never noticed.

Ángel started thinking about Iker, about the struggle he was undoubtedly having with his novel, and how he, Ángel, had not known how to help. Was it too late, he wondered. It was clear that his bright idea that poor Alcaén should serve as Iker's model for the story had so far been a total failure – not only had Alcaén not told Iker about his experiences with the advertisements for the non-existent houses but, on top of that, he had vanished; for the past couple of evenings he hadn't showed up, hadn't even bothered to phone. 'Damn fool,' he said to himself; then, arbitrarily linking this subject with the previous one: 'You wouldn't have such a weak character if you had been the son of Ramona Durango'; though this perhaps said less about what he thought of Alcaén than what he thought of himself: a tough, dynamic man, experienced in the ways of the world.

His thoughts returned to Iker; he saw him as a boy of sharp-featured, street-wise beauty; an intelligent young man, with good skills and bad luck, which he had undertaken to put right ever since the night, two years earlier, when they had met in the Sívori. He remembered their chance meeting, their first conversation, during which Iker had told him that he was about to finish his studies, and Ángel that his mother had just died.

'Ramona Durango . . .' said Iker, and looked at him rather uncertainly. 'That's a wonderful name. It sounds like . . . erm, it sounds like the name of someone very sweet and at the same time very strong.'

Ángel looked at him more closely, noting his rather disreputable nose, his penetrating greenish eyes; the ambushed look on his face, always slightly on the defensive. If at that moment he'd had to describe Iker in a word, for some reason that word would have been 'undergrowth'.

'What else? Tell me what else my mother's name suggests to you.'

'Let's see . . . Someone passionate, that's for sure. But also someone who's loyal, persistent, perhaps contradictory. That name would be a good starting point for a story.'

Ángel felt moved by what he heard. He was also impressed by the way Iker had guessed a great deal from very few facts.

'So you're a writer? Have you already had something published? If you have, I'd love to read it.'

The boy sketched an ironic smile. Ángel saw that he had extraordinarily white teeth.

'Who? Me? If only that were true. I'd love to have, but no, unfortunately.'

They discussed books, novelists, some ideas Iker had had for a couple of short stories. And from that moment on, Ángel involved himself more and more in Iker's projects; he suggested certain changes to things Iker was writing, he put in a good word for him with some of his private patients, among whom were two professors, a female publisher of children's books, and the deputy editor of a newspaper, who in the end offered Iker a small job: writing a daily twenty-line text about a writer of any era or nationality who had died on that very same day. 'Today marks seventy-five years since the death of the novelist Franz Kafka in the sanatorium in Kierling, on the outskirts of Vienna,' Iker would write. Or: 'It was 108 years ago today that Herman Melville, the creator of Moby Dick, passed away'; 'Today is the sixtieth anniversary of the death of the poet Antonio Machado, who died in the French city of Collioure'. And so on: Mark Twain died today, Isak Dinesen died today, Lope de Vega died today, Marguerite Duras died today, Samuel Beckett died today . . . They didn't pay him much, but Iker liked his work and took great pains to polish each one of his death notices, to build up little by little his exclusive and unusual cemetery. Sometimes, when someone asked him what he did for a living, he'd reply with a straight face: 'I disinter people.'

Of course, as well as having found him that job, Ángel Biedma often assisted in the search for characters, would pore over his books and encyclopaedias and draw up his own lists of candidates. But that wasn't all; he also liked to buy Iker the occasional present. It started with small practical gifts, such as a miniature Japanese tape-recorder so he could record sudden ideas, and then other, more personal items, especially clothes; at first it was just accessories like a scarf or a pair of leather gloves, and then, later, when they knew each other better, a sweater, a T-shirt and even, for his birthday, a coat. There were occasions, when Ángel saw him enter the Sívori kitted out with one or several of his gifts, that he felt a patriarchal sense of pride, akin to what a sculptor felt before a statue carved with his own hands.

But his influence had seemed to weaken as soon as Iker started to write the novel about the man who never appeared in his own dreams. It was a good story, and both of them thought it had the makings of something important. Apparently, they were both wrong.

Whether this was true or not, Ángel did not intend to give up. Sooner or later he would come up with a solution, of that he was sure.

He drank the milk, and went back to bed. Had he ever been in a swamp? Or in a white tower? Did he know a woman who wore a red skirt? Never sleep on your heart, because if you do, you'll dream of the Devil.

13

The Whole Truth

The taxi driver had the radio on, but Alcaén wasn't listening to it, for at that very moment he wasn't there, he was with Laura Salinas a half-hour later, in the bar-restaurant where they had arranged to eat, telling her about his feelings for her and about robbing the insurance company. Or maybe not. Maybe he wouldn't tell her about that. How would she interpret it? Would she consider it proof of his love or merely of his stupidity? In his mind he had seen her react to his story in a thousand different ways; in some versions she stood up from the table, screaming that she never wanted to see him again; in others, she threw herself into his arms, or laughed at him, cried with happiness, blamed herself, acted indifferent, slapped him. Which of all these premonitions was the right one?

At times he tried to focus his attention on the traffic or on the people in the streets, but the words Laura was going to say pursued him, breaking against him like waves against a pier, eroding him with their relentless water, their corrosive order.

He tried to escape from his fear, but he again started thinking about the night of the robbery at the insurance company – about how he had sat at home in his living room until dawn, feeling an endless sense of shame at the sight of the tools assembled for the raid: the overcoat with the double lining, the screwdriver, the rubber gloves, the bags of sand, the small jar with the blood; looking at them and no longer seeing them as pieces from the same puzzle but as unrelated objects whose sum total gave one result: Alcaén Sánchez was a coward.

I suppose you'll already have guessed why. I suppose you already know that he hadn't proved capable of taking the money from his office. He tried, but he couldn't. He had been there, he had gone to fetch his overcoat because the radiator wasn't working, he had put the cases on the desk and taken out the first wad of banknotes, ready to stash them away in his hidden lining. That had been it. Now, in the taxi that was taking him closer to the moment when he might lose Laura for ever, he reconstructed that afternoon, telling himself: 'I'm very nervous, my hands are shaking, the money looks different, it looks useless, abstract, I'm cold, there's a telephone ringing in the next room.' That was how he thought about it, in the present tense, the way in postcards you write, here it's very hot, the children go to bed late, Juan is out buying the papers, as if the person who'll receive it were right beside us, and not somewhere else, a fortnight later.

'For fuck's sake! This city!' said the taxi driver suddenly. 'Traffic in the morning, traffic at night; hold-ups from east to west and from Monday to Sunday. And it's gettin' worse and worse and worse . . . This country's completely hopeless, European Union or no European Union. I mean, come on! Germany's exactly like this?

Who made that one up? Or France; that France's like this? And you better hope there aren't any roadworks, cos otherwise this journey's gonna set you back 2,500. How far are we going to get at this rate, you tell me. And do you know whose fault it is? My wife reckons it's the mayor's, and I tell her: what the fuck's the mayor got to do with it, 'course it's not his fault, it's all your fault – you women. Don't believe me? Plain as day, I'm tellin' you. The husband comes along, buys his wife one of them 4 x 4s, bugger bicycles, and off these women drive safe as bleedin' houses in their whacking great jeeps and the rest of us can go pray; and don't give me that about machismo and all that crap, cos the trouble these women cause is goin' to go down in the record books, they don't know how to drive 'em, don't know how to park 'em, and count yourself lucky they don't ram into your back end and concertina your car, making you look like you're driving some Japanese model . . . the husband pays the taxes, the premiums, the licence and afterwards the damages – 6,000-odd pesetas an hour garages charge for labour these days. Am I right or am I right? Well, in that case, my friends, ban all Land Rovers, Nissans and all the rest of 'em, ban 'em, end of story, oh, I can understand the husbands, they got us into this mess, giving their women whatever they want just to get them off their backs, women give you a right earful when they want to, they start giving you the old story about how So-and-so's got one, So-and-so-other says it's much safer for the kids . . . Come on, who the hell could put up with that? A slave is what you are in the end; you can say what you

81

like, but when the missus arrives you might as well take a running jump. It's true, Bloody hell, you know it is, they're worse than the plagues of Egypt. Now then, if they want to drive, that's fine by me, I'd let 'em drive till they drop, but forget four-wheel drives, fuck that, delivery vans I'd give 'em, they want equality? Here, drive a Citroën, go unload meat at the slaughterhouse. And if not, go drive Formula One, go round the track at Jarama. That's what they should let 'em do – go smash themselves up like Niki Lauda, damn right, go kill themselves like Ayrton Senna, go get themselves picked out of the wreckage of their racing cars, have their pieces thrown to the dogs. They wanted equality, didn't they? Well, how about that for equality, bitch, how about that for equality!'

The taxi driver, whose greasy voice had gradually risen to a yell and who ended his tirade by slamming his fist on the steering wheel, had kept throwing him glances in the rear-view mirror, on the lookout for a show of complicity, until Alcaén gave a couple of nods of assent and then felt bad for not contradicting the man. Though, on the other hand, why bother to argue with a raving lunatic? What was that imbecile doing with his life? Alcaén studied him furtively: the man gave the impression of being cut in two, caught in mid-metamorphosis; the lower part wore trainers, diamond-patterned socks, and green stretch-nylon tracksuit trousers with white stripes; from the waist up, a dark-crimson knitted V-neck garment that vaguely resembled a shirt, an oil-blue jacket, and fingerless driving gloves. His face concealed no great mysteries, it looked like a half-carved bas-relief or a ship's figurehead worn down by the ocean. Alcaén felt like hitting the man. He didn't – he never did anything.

On reaching his destination, he paid the driver and went inside the restaurant. He made his way towards their table. Laura Salinas saw him coming, and he tried to detect a look of surprise or shock in her eyes, for that morning he was not in disguise, he was not wearing his rich man's suit or his designer sweater, only the clothes of the real Alcaén Sánchez: a jumper, a pair of jeans, a dark three-quarter-length coat.

'Hello,' he said. The girl looked at him somewhat surprised, though it was hard to know whether it was due to his devalued appearance or the seriousness in his voice.

'How are you?'

'Laura . . . listen to me carefully, there's something I have to tell you. I'm not the person you think I am.'

And he really did tell her who he was and how he had lied to her. He told her that he was not going to buy the house, that he was just a lowly clerk in an insurance company, and all the other things that you all already know. Laura Salinas acted as if it made no difference to her. He told her that he loved her with all his heart, and though she went back to behaving as normal, Alcaén sensed they were slowly drawing apart; he sensed a centrifugal force gradually, and irrevocably, taking him away from her. He tried reminding her of the times they'd had together, the meal in the Thai restaurant, the dinner at the racetrack. He tried to come up with something specific, some proof of the happiness she had felt, but without success. Then, as a last resort, he told her he had been on the point of robbing his insurance company, he explained his plan to her, trying to make her see it for what it was – an act born of sublime love. And then he fell silent. He sat there, expectant, unmoving, separated from her by an immense half metre.

'Poor old Alcaén, who was about to go to prison for my sake!' said Laura suddenly, violently throwing her head back and letting out a loud sarcastic laugh. She then took a packet of cheap cigarettes from out her handbag, and struck a match against the side of the table, dispersing the smoke with a swipe. Alcaén was surprised by these rather coarse actions, unbecoming of her. He remained silent, breathing in the air altered by the smell of tobacco and phosphorous. In front of him, Laura Salinas smoked on with uncouth, lavish gestures, staring into space, as if boasting of her lack of interest in what she'd just heard.

'Well,' said Alcaén, 'I can't think what else . . . I'm really sorry. You probably won't want to see me again.'

The woman gave him a look composed of malice, mockery and disbelief. Her eyes were no longer ochre, but yellow. As yellow as the tartness of a lemon or the twisting streak of a reptile.

'Probably? Listen, sunshine, you must be king of the optimists.'

That was it. That was all she said. Then she stood up and left.

For a few minutes, all around Alcaén the room seemed to cloud, as when sand is disturbed on an ocean floor. He had the impression that some of his senses heightened while others dissolved: on the one hand, he was receiving distant smells, muffled sounds and hazy outlines; on the other, he experienced the bitter taste of Laura's words and, in the pads of his fingers, he could feel their pain. A dry, burning pain.

He paid the bill, went out into the street, and walked for an hour until he reached his apartment. Laura Salinas had never set foot there and yet, the moment he walked in, it seemed abandoned, empty, as though she had just left it for ever. He switched on the television. There was a Frenchman who had recently had both hands transplanted; he was able to move his thumbs and his nails were starting to grow. What must you feel when you pick up a bottle or a fork with another man's hands? Or when you touch your own body? Alcaén Sánchez pressed his fingers to his face, changed channels, saw buildings wrecked by a tornado, two men boxing in a garage. Then he switched the television off.

And that could have been the end of this story. That image could have been the last one you saw of Alcaén, humiliated and alone, reduced once and for all to the narrow horizons of himself.

However, it isn't. Unfortunately, this is not where this story ends. At times, as one song says, that you've lost everything doesn't mean that you can't still lose a little more.

14

Poisoned Water

'A robbery?' Iker Orbáiz exclaimed. 'You were about to steal thirty million pesetas for her?'

'Yeah, well . . .' Alcaén replied, '. . . almost. But thank God I didn't have the guts. I didn't say anything to you before because . . . you know, seen from a distance it seems so ridiculous.'

Iker stared at him in astonishment, and, for some reason, Ángel Biedma looked angry. They were in the Sívori, and two weeks had passed since Alcaén Sánchez's last meeting with Laura Salinas; two weeks during which each of the three men had continued to go about his own business, but without making much progress.

Ángel had carried on working in the mornings at the hospital and in the afternoons at his private surgery; going out with Iker to dinner, to the cinema, to the bar; trying to find material for him, ideas that could be of use. Apart from that, he had suffered from terrible pains in his legs, because it had rained a lot and damp weather was very bad for him. As always when he was in that agony, he cursed the bastard who had provoked his misfortune, the cretin who caused the accident in Barcelona; he hoped he'd had a crash two days later, that stupid miserable son of a bitch; he hoped he'd had his brains splattered across a motorway. Ángel managed to get through his crisis with painkillers and steaming hot baths.

Iker, for his part, had carried on writing his brief obituary articles, and spent many hours thinking up and rejecting ideas for his story about the man who never appeared in his own dreams. In fact, though exhausting, his work was in vain – he kept digging but the hole got no deeper. He had hardly progressed from where his character poisoned an apple in a grocery shop. Should he have someone die? Should the newspapers splash it all over their front pages? He began to think seriously about giving up.

But just as he found himself at a dead end, the most unexpected thing happened: one night, Alcaén Sánchez reappeared at the Sívori and made a surprising confession, namely that he sometimes placed false advertisements in newspapers, adverts offering for sale houses that didn't exist, inviting potential buyers to vacant plots of land, areas of open ground or ruined buildings. Alcaén even showed him a cutting from a newspaper: 'House with four bedrooms, very spacious living room, dining room, fitted kitchen, two en-suite bathrooms, attic, double garage, 1,000m² of land.' Iker asked him why he did it and Alcaén replied that he wasn't really sure. Against whom were his actions directed? No one. What did he have to gain? Nothing; perhaps it was only a form of revenge for his bad luck, his lack of options. Sitting with them, on the other side of the table, Ángel Biedma was smiling peaceably, his eyes half-closed, his hands joined in a pose of absolute composure, of ecclesiastic serenity.

How incredible, thought Iker; it seemed an episode straight out of one of his stories. Naturally, he immediately began to feed it into his novel, in which Alcaén Sánchez before long not only summoned the buyers to an empty plot of land but also took to stationing himself in a nearby café, spying on them, and, on occasion, following them, recording their appearance and their addresses in a notebook. His catalogue grew; soon it included sophisticated women and confused men, neurotic female executives, angry office workers, married couples with children recovering from chickenpox. He hated them all, without exception. Poisoning an apple wasn't enough – he'd have liked to poison the city's water supply, finish them off in one fell swoop. He might just do it.

As for the real Alcaén Sánchez, he had led a miserable existence throughout those two weeks: he called Laura Salinas three or four times on her number at the estate agency, but they always gave him an excuse, saying she was in a meeting, that she was with a client, that it was her day off, that she was showing a house on the outskirts of the city. He didn't want to insist further, he thought it would serve no purpose; he retired to his previous life like someone falling back into a void after, for one brief moment, managing to clutch a branch, a ledge, a helping hand. He resumed going from his house to the insurance company and from there to the Sívori. He went back to visiting houses for sale, dressed in his disguise as a wealthy man. He also went to a museum and bought a postcard of that painting by Goya – Saturn devouring his son.

At last, that night, while he listened to Iker and Ángel have one of their usual conversations, and when both what had happened and what had been about to happen began to seem very distant, maybe even slightly unreal, he decided to tell his friends everything – encouraged perhaps by the success of that other story Ángel Biedma had thought up about the fraudulent adverts, or perhaps because he had decided to prove to them that the Alcaén Sánchez they saw was the tip of an iceberg, a wolf in sheep's clothing.

'And you were there shut up in the room where you count all the money, with the bags of sand, the false blood and everything else?'

Yes I was, he told Iker, who let out a whistle. Ángel Biedma did not seem so impressed.

'Anyway,' he said, gesturing with his restless hands, 'this plan of yours . . . has, how can I put it, many grey areas. For a start, the police would've put you under surveillance, assuming they didn't arrest you.'

'Arrest me? I don't think so. Actually, they may not even have suspected me. Don't forget that all the evidence led to a different man.'

'But you couldn't have used the money; the moment you bought the house, or anything like that, you'd have given yourself away.'

Alcaén lowered his gaze. He didn't like Ángel's tone of voice one bit.

'Not at first,' he said, 'but I could have a little later on. And, in any case, even if I didn't buy the house, I'd have had enough money to treat Laura like a queen.'

'OK, so your plan was perfect. Why didn't you go through with it, then?'

Alcaén bit his lip, ran his hand over the red velvet of the armchair, and looked away. Everything was in its place, Gloria behind the bar, washing glasses; the dartboard on the wall at the back, three darts stuck in; the amber mirrors and the ceremonial drinks, the photograph of T. S. Eliot and the green lamps. There was music playing: one of those jazz records that Ángel liked and that he gave to Gloria so she'd put them on when he was there; always saxophone players, men called Joe Henderson, Dexter Gordon, Gerry Mulligan, John Coltrane, Hank Mobley.

'I suppose . . . I don't know, I suppose I lack the courage to do something like that.'

Ángel Biedma looked at him the way you do a trophy. The way you regard a dam across a river, a city that has fallen.

'Courage,' he said. 'Yes, that is difficult to have. The rest is straightforward, but that's complicated.'

'Perhaps it's not a question of that,' Iker cut in. 'Maybe it's that, in the end, the girl wasn't that important to you. Or maybe it was just a game, like visiting houses for sale that you could never afford.'

'That's not true! I . . .' suddenly Alcaén felt a tightening in his throat, as if from a large invisible rope: again he saw Laura Salinas, saw her chestnut hair, her pale hands, her ochre-coloured eyes, her inestimable body. '. . . You don't understand . . . I'd have done anything for her.'

'Anything? No one can do anything – not for himself, not for anyone else,' said Iker.

However, he was looking at Alcaén in a way that was different. He was looking at him with respect. Alcaén wasn't a vet, nor did he want to poison the water supply of a city, he didn't exterminate pigeons, his father was a jeweller called Nicolás who didn't die locked away in his bedroom, nor had he copied every morning for years, without anyone knowing why, the list of the deceased from the newspaper. But, all at once, Alcaén Sánchez was someone to whom all this could have happened.

'Yes, no one can do anything,' Ángel Biedma then said. 'Except for a lunatic or a murderer.'

15

No Sunlight for You Tomorrow

On the left was a woman called Olga. When she was young her eyes had possessed a sort of exuberant sadness that moved all those who looked at her and made her very popular among the boys in her class. In those days, she had a capricious, childish character; she talked with wit and malice about her friends, and always dressed impeccably, with the kind of somewhat haughty elegance intended, in a sense, to put others down, make them seem scruffy and vulgar. At the age of thirty, having turned down a dozen others, she married a man with an angular face and stiff manner, who always wore grey and gave the impression of being caged behind an ever-present expression of grim displeasure. Olga's life filled with disappointments, her clothes went out of fashion, the light left her eyes and, in time, she even ceased to walk with her usual majesty, becoming hesitant, as if venturing over a gorge on a woodworm-riddled bridge. At first she had tried to adapt to her husband's steely character; she made an effort to bear her marriage with patience and good intentions; every Sunday she would go to church where, emboldened by the gold of the statues and the effusive scent of the incense, she would kneel at the feet of the priest and ask God to temper her husband's severity. But later, by then drowning in resentment and hatred, she asked God to kill him, to free her from such a cruel, inscrutable being. When the man did indeed die, from cancer, after they had been married for twenty years, she set about clearing out her life – she threw away his grey trousers and ties, she had the walls repainted and she bought herself a pair of orange shoes. A month later, as she was crossing a square in the vicinity of a market, on her way to meet up with some old friends in a bar, she was knocked down by a truck carrying cabbages. The cabbages spilled out onto the pavement, one of the orange shoes ended up in the narrow street behind the market, and there it remained, mixed in with the scraps of meat and vegetables and the empty crates, looking like some inedible species of fish or a strange tropical fruit.

On the right was a man called Manuel. He had always worked as a gardener. He drove a sit-on lawn-mower, trimmed back vines and Arizona cypresses, planted tulips or violets, and guided bunches of lilac over fences. At night, as he lay sleeping in the darkness of his home, he dreamed of smells: the climactic perfume of gardenias or honeysuckle, the cold-coffee aroma of damp earth. One July morning, while perched high up in an elm, he lost his balance and fell to the ground. The lady of the house heard the crash, thought someone had just jumped into the swimming pool, and went to the bathroom to fetch towels. His wife washed him and dressed him in the suit he had always worn for special occasions, but when he was buried, his fingers were still stained slightly green and there were bits of grass under his nails.

Iker Orbáiz knew all this about Olga Torres Martínez and Manuel Suárez Sandoval, the two people buried in the graves alongside his father's, because the families of the deceased had told him; they had told him in pained voices and with resigned gestures while arranging carnations or chrysanthemums on the tombstones – on afternoons when Iker went to that cemetery and stood at the graveside, remembering again his father's story. He saw unconnected scenes from his life with his father; moving, as it were, between the words his father had liked most – honesty, shame, unacceptable or dignity – like someone moving amid the rubble of a ruined house; or he recalled trivial details which, despite their triviality, had etched themselves on his memory as clearly as the inscriptions and epitaphs chiselled on the graves in the cemetery. He recalled his anger, his sense of duty and discipline, his intransigence; he recalled a blue-checked shirt and a cut-throat razor with mother-of-pearl handle, a Holy Week in Cádiz, and the day he turned ten: the moment when, that night, he got out of bed and saw his father in the room where they'd celebrated the party, saw him alone in the dark, among the balloons and the streamers, finishing off what the guests had left, pieces of cake and sandwiches, crisps, half-drunk bottles of Pepsi-Cola or Fanta. For some reason, for Iker that was his father, that man silently chewing the humble remains of the feast.

'My father's name was Aitor,' Iker told Ángel the night they met in the Sívori, after Ángel had told him about Ramona Durango. 'Aitor Orbáiz. He had such a scrupulous memory that when talking about something we'd done five or six years earlier he was liable to mention the weather and the clothes each of us had worn; he'd say: "You remember that time we ate quails in Segovia, in a restaurant near the aqueduct, one Sunday in October, it was pouring with rain and you were wearing a brown duffel coat, that one with the tartan lining we bought you for Christmas in a shop in Calle San Bernardo?"'

'Seriously?'

'He was a strange man. He loved finding out about the most absurd things and was always reading those little books that came in the *Enciclopedia Popular Ilustrada* series, about the pioneers of aviation; astrology, the Vikings, Australia, Hemingway, the Nuremberg trials, flying saucers . . .'

'Hemingway too?'

'Oh, yes. I remember a volume called *Hemingway the Magnificent*. I also remember other titles: *Hitler Didn't Die, Where is the Head of Francisco Goya?* Another was *Dalí isn't Mad*.'

'I think you're right: he was a strange sort.'

'He was forever talking about what he found in those little tomes. For example, he'd say to you: "Do you know just how many shipwrecks there have been throughout history?" And then he'd tell you how the *Empire Windrush* sank thirty miles off the coast of Algeria, the *Birkenhead* forty miles off Cape Town, the *Niagara* twenty miles from London; he'd tell you that the Captain of the *Titanic* was called Edward J. Smith; that the troopship *Lusitania* was torpedoed by a U-20 submarine in the English Channel . . .'

'And you still remember all that!'

'Sure. Listen: the German lieutenant Günter Prien was awarded the Iron Cross for sinking the *Royal Oak* and the *Repulse*, anchored in the Scapa Flow; the *Andrea Doria* was attacked by the *Stockholm* not far from New York; Japanese sailors ate *okashiratsuki* fish to ward off misfortune, but over a hundred of them died on the island of Gogo . . . What do you reckon? I bet you don't know many people who can remember the word *okashiratsuki*.'

'Bravo!' said Doctor Biedma, throwing up his hands and roaring with laughter.

'Well, the thing is that when my father turned sixty he became obsessive, first about saving energy, then about cleanliness. And, in the end, there was that business about the water.'

'What about the water?'

'He said that we didn't realise it, but that the world was becoming one gigantic desert and that we were wasting water not knowing how precious it was and, above all, not realising how precious it would become in the future.'

'Well, actually he was right. You can live without oil or a credit card, but not without water.'

'Yeah, true, but he became paranoid about it. He'd follow us around, making sure we didn't leave any taps on; he'd bang on the bathroom door whenever you took a shower, accusing you of wasting litres and litres of water; he'd stick up on mirrors cuttings from newspapers about droughts or about the shortage of supplies in our reservoirs;

he even began to check how much we drank at meal-times. Then he started to stockpile bottles. He filled up the refrigerator, the wardrobes, the cellar . . . Can you imagine? He even kept some in the boot of the car. There came a point when we actually started to feel afraid, all those plastic bottles seemed . . . I don't know . . . threatening, hidden behind the sofa, under the beds . . . Later on, my mother discovered that every night before going to bed he'd leave a knife under the mattress, to defend himself against any intruder who came to steal his water. For two years, he lived like that. In the end we put him in a home, and he died five months later. Have you ever been in one of those places? They're a sort of . . . I don't know, Purgatory. They're full of hopeless cases – most of them are like lost souls, alive only because they're not dead, but that's all. It's awful. What made a big impression on me was watching them eat. I wouldn't know how to explain it, but that's what struck me most – seeing them still eating in spite of everything, seeing them steal each other's piece of bread or fruit; their pointless greed, their instinctive appetite.'

'What did you do with the water?' Ángel asked. 'What happened to the bottles?'

Iker looked at him, confused.

'The water? Oh, we drank it. Actually, there's still a lot left.'

'Yes, that could be a good ending,' Dr Biedma murmured, 'the whole family around the table, staring at the glasses filled with that weird water. What I mean is, it would make a good ending if it were a story. Or maybe

97

this is better: in the last lines, the wife of the deceased is in the kitchen, lights off, emptying the bottles of water down the sink one after the other, listening to the sound the water makes as it disappears down the pipes.'

That was how his relationship with Ángel Biedma had started, and that was how it continued. Of course, to begin with, Iker mistrusted him greatly; he had been frightened by his attentiveness, his gifts, by the way he was interfering more and more with his life and his projects; by how he thought he could guide his tastes, his readings, his ambitions. On Iker Orbáiz Ángel Biedma had the contradictory effect of one of those sugary drinks which, instead of quenching thirst, cause it. But, little by little, Iker learnt how to handle him, how to balance his feelings towards him: to consider him by turns a friend and a meddler; to ignore most of his ideas, which often struck Iker as pretentious and useless, whilst at the same time enjoying his generous nature, good advice and their conversations in the Sívori. He was also grateful to Ángel for having recommended him to a number of people he knew, for helping to get him the job on the newspaper, those brief obituaries he so enjoyed writing and that had provided him with a fresh perspective: that of a person who knows that while, in the end, no life is so very different from any other, there are a thousand ways to die. Most people think the opposite is true. Most people are wrong. Aitor Orbáiz had died on the same day as the poet Azorín. Iker thought he would like to die on the same day as Marcel Proust. Or to die on 5 November, like Luis Cernuda.

Iker turned away from his father's grave and, as usual, he felt a sense of distaste as he walked back amid the mausoleums and the crypts, past the angels and the cypresses; a sensation similar to that of walking across a swamp, through mud and stagnant waters.

He started thinking of what Alcaén Sánchez had confessed to them, his outrageous plan to rob the insurance company, and of whether or not he should use this information in his novel about the man who never appeared in his own dreams. Maybe Ángel Biedma was wrong, Iker reflected, and that to base yourself on a real model when writing a book was a huge mistake: people are endless, hard to resolve.

He passed a woman carrying a bunch of white camellias, and a man counting something on his fingers – numbers? Syllables? He went into a bar, ordered a coffee, and felt an absolute aversion for the clients there at that time of the morning. Gross and vulgar people, he told himself, absolutely proud of their grossness and vulgarity. People who were in search of nothing; had no aspirations. 'Don't forget that, deep down, achieving things is easier than wanting them,' Ángel Biedma had once said to him.

Then he remembered a time his father, as a punishment, had not allowed him to see sunlight for a whole day; tomorrow you'll go to bed in the morning and stay awake at night, his father had told him, I hope that teaches you the value of things. What things had he been talking about? Iker couldn't remember. Perhaps that had been the day on which Aitor Orbaíz had started to go mad, to lose his way in the midst of his apocalyptic honesty, his irrevocable dignity, his stupid shame. And he thought too that perhaps, in a certain sense, it had also been the day on which he, Iker, had taken his first step towards Ángel Biedma, towards a man who would treat him with the consideration and the affection he felt he deserved. A powerful man, but one easily disarmed.

'You see?' he would have liked to say to his father. 'You never were either of those two things.'

16

The Second Time

Two weeks later, at the end of a Wednesday afternoon in early May, Alcaén was at his desk in the insurance company when his telephone rang.

'Hello?' he said, trying to make his voice sound curt, thinking it would be Virginia Urquijo, Señor Montero's secretary. He was wrong.

'Hi, Alcaén. It's Laura. Laura Salinas.'

A dense, oceanic silence formed, the sort you get if you press a sea shell to your ear. Then Alcaén started to hear his own heart; he felt it swell, brim over and flood the office, drowning out the sound of the conversations, the buzzers, the doors, the computers. Before replying, he tried to swallow; but he had no saliva, only a hot, thick tar.

'Laura . . . I thought you'd never speak to me again. I called you a few times, but they kept telling me . . .'

'I know you've called me. I also know that I trusted you and you lied to me.'

Her voice was different, not that it had changed but it conflicted with the one he remembered; it had darkened and was more intransigent, more austere; so much so, that it made him picture her as sturdier, taller, less young; her voice made him think of a woman who was sad, the same way an empty cathedral puts you in mind of a vanquished god.

'Forgive me,' he answered, in a whisper. 'I wish I hadn't.'

'Yes, I wish you hadn't.'

'I'm very sorry, Laura.'

'You know what? I'm sorry too. I'm sorry I met you.'

'Please don't say that.'

'It's the truth. I swear to God I'm sorry I ever met you. But at the same time . . .' there was a pause, which he did nothing to break: he preferred to wait for events, to see where those words would lead. '. . . At the same time, I'm also sorry I lost you.'

Her breathing sounded laboured; through the earpiece it came in bursts, its cadence irregular, as if she were crying. Alcaén wondered if that phrase meant what he thought it meant. Desperately he searched for a way to find out, a means by which to probe.

'But, Laura, that's not true. If you had wanted . . .'

'No, you're wrong. You don't know anything, Alcaén, you don't know anything about my life.'

'But I know something about my own: I know it has no meaning without you.'

'Jesus Christ! Where did you get that one from? A soap opera? Don't try to trick me, I'm warning you. Once was already more than enough.'

Alcaén looked around him: how strange it all seemed, the filing cabinets, the employees, the fluorescent strip lights, the desks, the wastepaper baskets. In his chest his heart was beating wildly.

'Listen, maybe it'd be better if we met up and talked. What's your answer?'

'Impossible. You don't know what you're asking.'

'Please, Laura. Just a couple of hours, any time you like, even today if you want, this evening.'

'This evening! No, that's out of the question. And what's more, you don't know that I . . . You don't know that I also . . . Look, Alcaén, I'm going to hang up now. Goodbye . . .'

'Wait!'

There was another silence. Then, Laura Salinas finished what she had begun to say.

'. . . that I also didn't tell you the truth.'

'I don't care. I don't know what you're referring to, and I don't care. You hear me? Laura, have dinner with me tonight, we'll go to the . . .'

'No, not tonight. I couldn't, even if I wanted to.'

'Tomorrow, then. We'll go to the Thai restaurant. Remember it? Say yes, Laura, give us both another chance.'

A further pause. Alcaén looked at the clock on the office wall: six o'clock and twenty-seven seconds, and twenty-eight, and twenty-nine, half past six. Had she hung up? Thirty-one, thirty-two, thirty-three.

'All right,' Laura said. 'Wait for me there, at around two. But I'm not promising. Understand? I can't guarantee I'll be there.'

The line went dead, and for a few minutes he was blank, absent, feeling as empty as an insect a spider had sucked dry. Then, he started to come to; little by little, he got over his surprise, straightening back up until he was Alcaén Sánchez once more, just like in those illustrations of evolution in which monkeys slowly progress into men, from *Australopithecus* via *Homo habilis*, and from there to *Homo erectus*, Neanderthal man, *Homo sapiens*, Cromagnon man . . . He turned his thoughts to the following afternoon. Which was better: to go dressed in his normal clothes or in his rich man's suit? Was it better with or without the packet of cigarillos? Should he perhaps take her some flowers? What sort of flowers?'

The telephone rang again. He pounced on it.

'Yes?'

'Virginia Urquijo speaking. Kind of you to spare the time, Señor Sánchez, you must be so busy. The boss has been expecting you for the past fifteen minutes, so unless you have any objection . . . But do take your time, please don't hurry, we wouldn't want you to fall over.'

He didn't even bother to answer. Where would that get him? What was the point? He filed some dossiers and some claim forms, tidied his desk and put away the stapler, Sellotape, pencil sharpener, pencils and letter-opener; he noted a couple of things down in his diary and, finally, began to make his way, as he did every afternoon, towards the director's office. Except that afternoon was very different. Awaiting him were the safe, the bullet-proof cases, the day's takings, the wads of blue, red and green banknotes. What were they exactly? What importance did they hold? Why did people fight for them, suffer for them; kill and let themselves be killed for them? This was an unusual world: in Geneva a man passed himself off as a doctor for eighteen years before murdering his wife, two children, parents and dog; in Paris, a mutilated man had been given the hands of a corpse, already he could move his fingers, his nails were growing; on Alcaén Sánchez's planet, Laura Salinas had left for ever, but now she was back. That was all that mattered.

17

Dragons and Pagodas

At half past two he poured himself another glass of wine, lit a cigarillo, looked at the prices in the menu, walked over to the door of the restaurant, went downstairs to the bathroom, counted the money he had on him, brushed his teeth with a travel toothbrush and went back to his table. It was the fourth time he had done all this. 'She's not going to come,' he told himself. 'I'm sure she's not going to come.'

By three o'clock the empty plates had turned into discs of ice, pieces of gravestone, stopped clocks. The waiting staff were giving him impatient looks and he, in an attempt to justify himself, had to grit his teeth and smile back at them, seek their patience and understanding by means of some coded gesture – a shrug of the shoulders and a curving of the lips, or a slow raising of the eyebrows and hands: see, this is what you get with women, I've been waiting for her for over an hour, what do you want me to do about it? The personnel of the restaurant consisted of two or three young men with Asiatic cheekbones and samurai physiques, five or six waitresses in blue kimonos and Chinese clogs, and a couple of manageresses with the airs and grace of geishas. The men had on sandals and wide-legged cotton trousers; the women wore their hair up in an oriental bun pierced through by long, slender batons of orange wood. Their faces bore signs of indifference and their clothes: metaphorical birds and sacred mountains, red dragons and pagodas.

At twenty past three Laura walked in. She wore sunglasses, a bone-coloured overcoat, an olive-green jumper and a denim skirt. She had on the same lipstick as on the first day, a shade between brown and cherry. Alcaén experienced a kind of giddiness, his stomach cramped; he felt that same mix of excitement and unease as someone surging down a roller coaster or circling high on a big wheel. She greeted him, extending her hand.

'Hello, Laura. You look . . . you're so beautiful.'

With a brusque, imperative gesture she cut him short.

'Alcaén, I've only come to say goodbye. That's all. OK? I don't want you to imagine anything different.'

Her words sounded rehearsed; they wanted to seem mature and irrevocable.

'To say goodbye? But I thought you weren't angry with me any more!'

'You're right: I'm not. I can't be angry with the person who's treated me better than anyone else in my life.'

'So what's the problem? I love you with all my soul. I lied to you because I thought . . . well, I thought that you'd . . .'

'You thought that I'd what? Say it, Alcaén. What did you think? That it was a question of money? Did you think I was for sale? That that's why I was seeing you – for a free meal in a place like this or a trip to the races?'

'Of course not! I just . . . I thought a woman of your sort wouldn't take any notice of someone like me.'

'You have no idea what sort of woman I am. You think you do, but you don't.'

'I know I'm crazy about you, and that's all I need to know.'

'You're crazy about someone who doesn't exist; a woman you've dreamt up.'

One of the geishas came over to take their order, and – not to waste time over such petty details – they asked for the set menu. While the manageress stood by their table, Alcaén noticed how Laura Salinas avoided looking up at her or saying a word, as though she were afraid of being spied on or of being given away by a confidante. But given away to whom and why?

Laura poured herself a glass of wine, and took off her jumper. Underneath she wore a tight-fitting lilac T-shirt, with short sleeves and V-neck; she wasn't wearing a bra and her breasts stood out; small yet firm, they swung when she moved, with a maritime roll. For an instant he stared at them, entranced, then looked away at her arms, which were very slender, and at her wrists, which were delicate and slightly flattened. On the fourth finger of her left hand there was a wedding ring.

The sight of it literally blinded Alcaén. Inside himself he felt a sudden thump, a jolt like the recoil from a weapon. Had the ring always been there? Was it possible that until that moment it had escaped his notice? With an anxious hand he stroked his throat, as if instead of a ring around the woman's finger there was a rope around his neck. Laura's eyes, too, were fixed on the wedding ring.

'Tell me he's dead,' Alcaén said, attempting to draw strength from weakness. 'Tell me you still wear it, but that he no longer exists. Or that it's not actually yours, it's only a family heirloom.'

She gave him a sweet, imploring smile, the kind you give to children or people you fear.

'No, Alcaén, I can't tell you that. I am married. I wish I wasn't.'

After these words there followed silence, a sepulchral silence, made of seconds and minutes that crystallized before his very eyes like rocks of quartz.

A pair of waiters brought their food, and one of the girls in a kimono lit a candle. One of the diners at the next table knocked over a glass of water; another had earrings in the shape of dolphins. The light in the room was dim and liquid. The air smelt of sandalwood.

'You're married, but you're here,' thought Alcaén, to encourage himself. 'You said earlier that I had . . .'

'Forget that,' she interrupted him. 'Forget about what I said or didn't say, whatever it was. Don't let yourself get more hurt – and don't hurt me, that's all I ask. Anything else is impossible.'

'. . . You said I had treated you better than anyone else in your life.'

She looked away and stared down at the floor.

'That's true; but what does it matter? Alcaén, I'm going to leave now.' She began to gather up her things, the sunglasses, the olive-green jumper, the overcoat; she leant slightly forwards, pushing back her chair and placing both palms on the table, ready to stand up.

'What does it matter? For Heaven's sake, Laura! The truth always matters.'

He reached out to clasp one of her hands; at first she not only left it there, but stared down, astonished and incredulous, at the form that resulted from those inert, interlocked fingers – as if it were some kind of incredible animal, a mutation, or a creature discovered in the depths of the ocean or on an archaeological dig – but then she did respond to his caresses. Suddenly, though, she pulled her hand away and said:

'I'll say it again: meeting you was the worst thing that ever happened to me.'

And rising brusquely to her feet, she looked at him, her eyes full of rage and tears, then she turned on her heels, and rushed out of the restaurant as if the devil were after her.

18

The Two Blue-eyed Children

'I've never told you the story of my father,' Ángel Biedma said.

'No,' Iker Orbáiz replied, 'you never have.'

'It's like something out of Tolstoy, you know? Or Galdós; yes, more like Pérez Galdós. To tell it properly you need to cover a lot of ground and have a lot of time; you need to start from the day the main character is born and continue right up until the day he dies.'

'Sounds good. Let's hear it.'

'All right. My father was called Gabriel and he didn't resemble anyone; he was born without any of the physical attributes of his family, who came from Granada and had the traits of certain Andalusians: Arab eyes and dark skin, an aquiline nose and jet-black hair, a weak jaw and thick stubble.'

'What do you mean exactly by Arab eyes?'

'Well, a lot of things, actually. I mean that they were intelligent, that's for sure, and also that they were . . . let me find the right word . . . It has to be one that makes you to think of, for example, mist . . . clouded maybe. I don't know . . . it's hard to say.'

'How about mist-veiled? Intelligent, mist-veiled eyes.'

'Perfect! Anyway, the point is that Gabriel was born with very pale-blue, almost sky-blue eyes, and hair that was radically blond – not the sort of straw blond you get in Spain, but a Nordic blond, a foreign whiteness.'

Ángel paused, lit a cigarette, took a couple of puffs without inhaling the smoke and passed it to Iker. If that was smoking, then catching flies in the garden is a safari hunt.

'What happened after that?'

'He looked so extraordinary in that environment that right from the first everyone treated him as if he were special – someone superior, infallible, predestined for success.'

'And of course, as a result, that's how he himself began to behave.'

'That's right. Things revolved around him with an unquestionable naturalness, and it seems that, for his part, the boy did show an astonishing maturity. In fact, it has to be said that he was number one at everything, whether at home, at school or in sport.'

'He never had rivals? No one tried to challenge him or to, so to speak, topple him?'

'Apparently not. It seems that, quite simply, he liked to be the general and the others liked to be his soldiers. That's all there was to it.'

'A lucky guy.'

'You can say that again. Then, when Gabriel was eleven years old, something happened which by that stage no one was expecting: his brother was born. They named him Ernesto.'

'Did Ernesto also have blond hair and blue eyes?' asked Iker, who was starting to show an interest in his friend's story. Ángel Biedma must have noticed it, for he gave a greedy smile and, with theatrical solemnity, paused for a few seconds, before proceeding.

'He did. Can you imagine? It was a mystery – people couldn't understand where that species of blond children had come from, and how it had reached my family. Perhaps they were descended from some hidden ancestor. Or perhaps Gabriel and Ernesto's parents would go on multiplying that species and soon there'd be an entire battalion of wonderful, indestructible children, wise children who were always right, golden-haired blue-eyed conquistadors to avenge that line of labourers and emigrants, men and women long used to humiliation and defeat.'

Iker Orbáiz laughed because Ángel had said these last phrases in a melodramatic, grandiloquent tone of voice, like an announcer on a government-sponsored newscast.

'Did Ernesto take Gabriel's place? Did he find out that his brother was his number one enemy? In which case that would make it a biblical story.'

'Yes, maybe so. In any case, there are many different accounts of this. They say that from the moment Ernesto was born, Gabriel became his companion and guardian, that he monopolised him and looked after him with total devotion, boundless affection: he fed him, bathed him, took him out for fresh air by the river Darro, along the Paseo de los Tristes, to the Plaza Nueva. And he went on doing this until the baby was three. By which time, Ernesto had become the spitting image of Gabriel, there was no denying it; he had the same features, the same look in the eyes; but also his intelligence, his mannerisms. Let me put it like this, Ernesto was on his way to being Gabriel, if you see what I mean; let's say that he was somehow gradually becoming his brother. And that's when it happened.'

Ángel Biedma paused once more, drank a sip of water and rubbed his legs which, as always at this time of day, were painful, particularly his knees.

'When what happened?' said Iker, moving Ángel's hands away and starting to give him a gentle massage himself.

'No one ever found out. One evening, Gabriel came home and said that Ernesto had fallen into the Darro from the edge of the Plaza Nueva. The child was dead, of course.'

'Bloody hell! He killed him?'

'Like I said, no one ever found out. Some say he did and some believe the opposite; some maintain they saw Gabriel push Ernesto, others swear they saw him fall into the river on his own.'

'What's your father's side of the story?'

'There isn't one. He never mentioned anything about this for as long as he lived. I found out about it after he died. But, actually, it's hard to accept that the Gabriel I knew and the Gabriel in the story were ever at any point the same person.'

'They were so very different?'

'My father was a failure. Take my word for it, he was nothing like his legend. Apparently he was never the same again after the death of Ernesto; he slowly dissolved. At fourteen he was less agile and less exceptional than he had been at thirteen, and even less so at fifteen, at sixteen. He didn't look after himself, he overate and began to put on weight, to lose his blue-eyed features and his attractive figure.'

'As if he was intent on destroying himself. Like someone taking a hammer to a statue of a god.'

'But here's the strangest part: on entering puberty, as you'd expect, he started to get facial hair, like everyone else; his beard and moustache appeared, and he let them grow. But guess what this beard and moustache were like. Black! As black as coal! And later on, when he turned twenty-five or twenty-six, he lost his hair. So you see: the blond boy was gone for ever, just as if Ernesto had been pulling him towards his grave. You know what I think? That you should use Gabriel in your novel.'

'You wouldn't mind?'

'Of course I wouldn't mind. In fact, maybe that way his life wouldn't have been so useless after all.'

'All right, in that case, I will.'

'Good, Iker, do it. Make him into Alcaén Sánchez's father, suggest that the events I've told you are the reason why that poor man ends up shut away in his room and copies out every day the list of the dead from the newspaper. That was already a fabulous idea and, with that background, it'll seem even more so.'

'Can I ask you one final question? What about your mother? When your parents met, did Ramona Durango already know that story?'

'Not only did she know it, but I think that was what

she loved about him. I'm pretty certain she believed that she would set the real Gabriel free, that she was going to rescue him from the bottomless pit of himself; from his ordinary looks and his mediocre job in a sub post-office. She wasn't able to, of course: after they'd been together ten years, she threw him out. I was nine, and from then on we were on our own, her and me.'

'Do you know what happened to him?'

'He went back to Granada. Retired. Died of cancer. Nothing extraordinary.'

'Tell me something. Do you really think Gabriel murdered Ernesto? Do you think that the man you knew was brave enough to commit a crime?'

'Sure he was; anyone can reach that point. Why not? It all depends on how far circumstances push you, and on what you think they're going to take from you. It depends on what life puts in your hand. It's that simple. If it hands you a spoon, you stir the coffee, and if it hands you a gun, you take a shot.'

19

A Word Bigger Than the Word Fear

Finally, after five days, Laura took his call. Until then, Alcaén had been phoning her every morning and afternoon, yet however much he insisted he always received the same replies: she's in a meeting, she's with a client, today's her day off, she's showing a house on the outskirts of the city. This time was different:

'Hello?'

'Hello, Laura, it's me, Alcaén. I need to see you. Please.'

'What? Are you crazy? No – no way. I thought I made it clear to you the last time. We can't ever see each other again. It's dangerous. Too dangerous,' she was speaking in a whisper and sounded as if she were frightened.

'I'll wait for you in the Bar Vizcaya, in one hour. Do you know where it is?'

'Yes, I do. But I'm not coming.'

'Laura, listen to me: I love you. You hear me? I don't know what's going on with you, I don't know exactly who you are or what your life is like. I know nothing about you, except the only thing that matters to me. I love you. I'd die for you.'

A vast, terrifying silence formed. The silence of an empty palace.

'Don't do this to me, Alcaén. Not if I really matter to

you as much as you say I do. I'm asking you – please stay away from me.'

'I'll be at Bar Vizcaya in an hour. Waiting for you.'

'You'll regret this, Alcaén. I'm warning you: if I go there, you'll regret having forced me.'

'No I won't. Whatever happens, I won't.'

Laura hung up. I don't know if anyone has ever put the phone down on you like that, and in circumstances more or less equivalent to his. If they have, you'll know how Alcaén Sánchez felt at that moment, the kind of anguish that filled his heart with mud, his mouth with ice, and his mind with flames; but if this has never happened to you, you'll be unable to understand, because you don't have the imagination and nor I the words able to explain it. If you can think of any, let me know, find one that's much stronger than uncertainty, twice as big as desperation, twice as big, even, as fear, and that will be the precise term, that will certainly be what we are looking for.

Alcaén switched the lights off in his apartment and left, all ready to set the course of his life, settle his destiny. It was a comfortable spring day, one of those when the world resembles a stage set and tragic stories seem inconceivable. The sky was fading gently, reducing the vigour of things little by little: it was that time of day when lights dull and sounds become muffled; when shops start to close and, in homes, there are lit fires and running baths, there are silent men in shirtsleeves, there are liquids on the boil and tired women, there are children slowly taking off their uniforms.

It may be that Alcaén dallied a little; that, impercepti-
bly, he adjusted to the stillness of his surroundings while
he wondered if afterwards, when in time he came to look
back, these things would be all there was before he won
Laura over or all there was before he lost her; because he
found that when he reached the Bar Vizcaya, the woman
was, quite unexpectedly, already waiting for him. She
wore the same sunglasses as on the previous occasion,
though at this time of day they were quite unnecessary;
also, Alcaén noticed that she had her right arm in a sling,
her hand was bandaged and her little, ring and middle
fingers were in a splint.

'But . . . what happened?'

'It's nothing, just an accident.'

'An accident? Tell me, Laura. Tell me what kind of
accident. What's wrong with your eyes? Why are you
wearing sunglasses?'

'The light bothers me.'

'Oh my God, he's beaten you up! That bastard has
beaten you up!'

'What are you saying?' Laura glanced left and right, as
if afraid someone might overhear them. 'No, Alcaén, I
fell in . . . I was in the kitchen . . .'

'It was my fault, wasn't it? That's it: your husband beat
you up for seeing me. I've been so stupid! Now I understand why you were afraid, why you said it was dangerous to meet.'

'Please, that's enough, don't say any more. I already
told you that it was impossible, I told you you had to forget me.' Alcaén saw that she was trembling violently: she

reached out for the cup that was beside her and spilled half the coffee onto the saucer.

'Let's go straight to a police station. We're going to report that bastard.'

'Are you out of your mind? Report him! He'd kill me. You don't know what he's like. Stay out of this, Alcaén. Don't call me again. Listen, it's the best thing you can do for me.'

'Come with me,' he said to her, taking hold of her uninjured arm. 'Come to my apartment with me, don't go back to that animal. The police will protect you; I'll be with you.'

'Protect me! Don't you read the newspapers?' She leant towards him, as if about to tell him a secret; she spoke in a low voice, into his ear, her words tense, full of odd intonations and broken glass. 'What kind of protection d'you think they'll give me? Every day some woman gets murdered in this country; stabbed or thrown off a balcony or burnt alive; killed by a man she's reported ten, fifteen times. The police take their statements, and then send them back home for the man to finish the job. Alcaén, I beg you: forget about me; it's what's best; what's safest.'

'Bastard!' Alcaén repeated. 'Bloody coward!' and as he said this he lost control, his eyes filled with tears. He wanted to take hold of her free hand but she pulled it back, horrified.

'No, my darling, you can't . . . I don't . . . I don't love you, you hear me? I don't love you!'

She turned, just like she'd done in the restaurant the last time, and she tried to flee, but this time Alcaén went after her.

They crossed a couple of streets that appeared chaotic, incomprehensible, the way a city is seen through the eyes of someone running, someone pelting down crooked pavements, amid illogical forms and toppling buildings. He caught up with her beside a doorway.

'My darling,' Alcaén said, gasping conspicuously from the exertion, 'you called me my darling.'

'No I didn't, that's a lie. You don't know what you're saying, you misheard me. Go away, Alcaén; go back to your life. I'm taking a big risk . . . If he saw us together . . .'

'I'd kill him. If he lays another finger on you, I'll kill him.'

'Shh! Don't say that. Don't ever say that again. Please, Alcaén, for all our sakes, let me go.'

Laura Salinas reached out her free hand, dried the tears on his face with her palm. Alcaén tried to kiss her; she didn't let him, she turned round again, was about to walk off but stopped, then came back, let him put his arms round her but when he tried to kiss her again, she denied him her mouth, retreating a few steps; then she moved towards him, grabbing hold of his jacket and drawing him into the doorway, and, this time, she did allow Alcaén the path to her lips, but only for a few instants, maybe four or five seconds, before taking a step back, abruptly shoving him away.

'No!' she said. 'No . . . I'm frightened.'

But she threw herself into his arms again, opening her jacket and taking Alcaén's hand, guiding it to her breasts; she kissed him with sweet savagery, with thirsty desire, biting his lips desperately, until he bled. Then she pulled away from him, brought a handkerchief up to her lips; staring at that bright red viscous liquid, she said: 'If only it were true; my God, if only he were dead.'

20

The Third Apple

'Alcaén Sánchez sat in darkness in the living room of his home, trying to recollect a particular day of his life,' Iker Orbáiz wrote.

That morning he had murdered three dozen pigeons in the gas chamber and, as always when that happened, he now felt ill at ease, somehow tarnished.

He did not want to think about the luxury homes he visited at weekends, about the adverts for non-existent houses, or about his father typing out the names of the deceased in the newspaper: Manuela García Puigcerdá, 85; José Francisco Azpeitia Ferrer, 79; Carlos Riquelme Urdiales, 62 . . . He did not want to think about any of that, he just wanted to sit there, very still, amid the spoilt air of his apartment, trying to piece back together an entire day of his life. That was what he had been doing, though he would have been hard-pressed to say why.

'On my tenth birthday, my mother gave me a bicycle,' he recalled. 'That morning I woke up very early, before dawn. My bedroom wall was painted sky-blue. It was a rainy day, I think. The bicycle was in the kitchen, it was green. My mother came up behind me, rubbing her eyes with her fists, and said: "Look who's up early today!" At half past eight, Uncle Luis rang.

For breakfast I had a cup of Cola-Cao and some fried bread. And yes, it was raining, the street smelt of acacias and wet tiles; over the damp asphalt the car tyres made the sound of razor blades' – he added little by little, meticulously, as if it were essential to reconstruct that lost world down to its smallest detail, before daring to put in place the characters who inhabited it.

For hours he carried on like this, sitting in the dark and reliving that day, not knowing if many of his memories were real or if he had made them up. The air in the room was becoming increasingly unbreathable: he had gone back to the grocer's where he had poisoned the apple, had looked for it without success and, in the end, he had bought them all; they came to eight kilos, and there they were, in his kitchen, invading the apartment with their smell of rust, of death.

'In the afternoon we loaded the bicycle into the boot of the car, and my father drove me into the countryside. He had put on a pair of khaki-coloured corduroy trousers, and I wore an anorak. I fell off two or three times, my knees got blood on them and grains of sand, they looked like a fruit sliced in two. While he watched me, my father jingled some coins in his pocket, as he almost always did.'

Alcaén broke off to go to the kitchen. He stared at the apples, wondering which one had the poison. There must have been thirty-five, forty apples there. In the course of that afternoon he had eaten two. He picked up a third and bit into it, slowly. Then he went back to his chair and turned on the television. On

124

*screen, an Argentinian psychoanalyst told how for
years he had treated a female patient who, at each ses-
sion, kept describing how she was going to accost
Borges in a street in Buenos Aires: once a day, always
at the same time, the woman would see him pass the
windows of the café where she had sat herself to wait
for him, thinking about how to approach him, what
she would say first.*

*'One of the times I fell the front light of the bike
got smashed,' Alcaén thought. 'My father called me an
idiot. At eight, it began to rain again, but then it
stopped. We went back home. When it got dark, I met
up with some friends on an area of waste ground; they
had made a bonfire from cardboard boxes and newspapers, and we ran, jumping through the fire. At the
instant you passed through the flames, you felt a sensation as if you were sinking into hot water.'*

Iker Orbáiz re-read these paragraphs. He wondered if his
character was going to die from that apple. He wanted to
describe the way that memories reached Alcaén, and, in
his mind, he had an image: a plague of locusts, thousands
and thousands falling from the sky onto a harvest.

Then he put some clothes on and went out, headed for
the Sívori, taking his chapter with him to show Ángel
Biedma.

How would Alcaén die? What would his last gesture be?
Iker thought about the writers in his obituaries. Pessoa
had died on 29 November; Neruda on 23 September,
Marguerite Yourcenar on 17 December. Pessoa had had
cirrhosis, Neruda, cancer; Marguerite Yourcenar had had

a brain haemorrhage. Pessoa died in Lisbon, Neruda in Santiago de Chile, Marguerite Yourcenar in the United States, on Mount Desert Island. Pessoa's hospital was called San Luis de los Franceses; Neruda's, the Santa María clinic; Marguerite Yourcenar's was the Bar Harbor sanatorium.

Did all that really hold any meaning? Iker wondered; did it contain some form of explanation? Pessoa had written down on a piece of paper, 'I know not what tomorrow may bring', and the following evening at eight o'clock he went blind, and murmured, 'Hand me my glasses.' Neruda woke with a start, ripping his pyjama jacket off, shouting: 'They're shooting them! They're shooting them!' Marguerite Yourcenar thought she was at the theatre watching Mishima's *Madame de Sade*; she expressed a couple of opinions about the actors, and applauded at the end of the first and second act; suddenly, she had drawn a sharp breath and opened her eyes wide, as if she had seen something rushing at her.

Iker was thinking about all this when he opened the door to the Sívori.

21

Shipwrecked on Tauris

He was a man of medium height with a poor complexion; he had a long face, a thin neck, gnarled hands. Alcaén took in these details as he followed him – as he had done every afternoon that week – to the train station. He hated every movement of that repulsive man, that despicable creature who beat Laura at night, who had deliberately broken three of her fingers, who often raped her – Laura Salinas herself had told him this, she'd told him in an awful monotone: sometimes he gets home in the middle of the night, reeking of alcohol; he knocks me out of bed, grabs me by the hair and forces me onto my knees, take my cock out, you whore, he tells me; the more I cry the harder he hits me; suck it, go on, bitch, scream and I'll kill you.

They got onto the same carriage of the train. Laura Salinas's husband was staring out of the window, staring at the darkness of a tunnel. Alcaén closed his eyes and saw him arrive home, saw him hitting his wife – some nights, when he's very drunk he likes to leave the curtains open and the lights on, so the neighbours can see us, put it right in, bitch; scream and I'll kill you.

Alcaén had his right hand in his pocket and wore a latex glove. He touched the monkey wrench he'd bought in a DIY store along with other items, so that it would pass unnoticed; he had handled it by the cardboard sheath around the wide end, and had made sure that the checkout operator who scanned it left her fingerprints on the handle; her prints that were plain arch or tented arch, accidental or plain whorl, double loop or central pocket loop.

Laura Salinas's husband was called Antonio Vázquez, and he owned a lottery outlet, a tiny place where customers could buy pools coupons, tickets for various lotteries, that sort of thing. It was there that Alcaén had seen him the first time; he had walked into the shop, picked up a pools coupon and begun to study the man while filling in the boxes: Real Madrid to beat Santander; Barcelona to beat Celta; Deportivo de La Coruña to draw against Valencia; Valladolid to lose against Athletic de Bilbao. He searched his face for the telltale signs of a monster, the attributes of an executioner, the traces of evil. Alcaén felt repulsed by the man's sallow complexion, nauseated by his greasy hair, his foul, saffron-coloured teeth. He wondered how Laura Salinas could have ended up in the power of a man like that; and he wondered, too, if he really wanted to know the answer.

The second time, he had followed the man from his office, noting the route he took to go home to the working-class area where they lived, in a red-brick building that Alcaén contemplated in a blind rage: that's where you batter her, you bastard, that's where you humiliate her, perhaps that's what you'll do again tonight, turn around, bitch, switch the light on, report me and I'll rip your guts out, slash your face.

The train was approaching Antonio Vázquez's stop. By the time it arrived it would be approximately a quarter to nine. At nine o'clock, Alcaén was expecting a call from Ángel Biedma on his mobile phone; before leaving the insurance company, he had told Ángel to ring him at home at precisely that time, because he wanted to tell him about the false advertisements they'd placed in the newspapers. Ángel would dial the number of his apartment, where Alcaén had activated the call transfer service so calls would be re-routed to his mobile. He checked that he had it with him, and that he also had a small tape recorder, which was the second part of his ploy.

The train drew to a halt. Antonio Vázquez alighted along with the other passengers and Alcaén followed. Now Vázquez would cross the station hall, walk as far as a small square and, from there, head for a public park that was almost always deserted, at the centre of which rose the statue of a goddess, which he entered every evening through a side gate and left via the entrance open on the other side. This time he didn't: he had gone no more than forty steps when Alcaén Sánchez attacked him from behind, striking the back of his head with the iron wrench, and, when he fell to the ground, barely making a sound, Alcaén went on striking him again and again, spitefully, viciously.

'Want someone to suck it now, do you, you big son of a bitch?' he spat at the body that lay at his feet now emptied of life, before throwing his weapon down alongside it.

He hurried back, retracing his steps to the train station. He looked at the time: nine o'clock already, he needed to get to a phone box, to shut out the sound of the street when Ángel Biedma called. Fortunately, the phone box was empty. At two minutes past nine, his mobile rang. Alcaén played the cassette on which he'd recorded some TV ads and held it up to the mouthpiece.

'Hello? Oh, hi there, Ángel! Christ, you're punctual, it's two minutes past nine,' he emphasised. 'Wait a second, let me turn the volume down on the television. Listen, how about meeting at the Sívori right now? Yes, just you and me, of course. No, I don't think Iker noticed either. No need to thank me, I'm always at your service. OK, in that case I'll have a shower and be on my way.'

'Thanks very much for the alibi, dummy,' he said mentally to Ángel Biedma, as he stopped a taxi to take him to Gloria's bar. Before going inside he'd stop off at a toilet somewhere, wet his hair in the washbasin and turn up at the Sívori fresh from a shower he never took, straight from a home where he hadn't been but one where, if need arose, Ángel would testify he had telephoned him on the night of the crime: oh yes, I remember it well, it had just gone nine o'clock; no, no, I'm sure, it was me who called him, he was at home watching television.

It was easy to kill a man, Alcaén reflected. It was even easy to forget. He did not feel good, but nor did he feel guilty; he had carried out an act of justice, like shooting vermin or crushing an insect. To him the only truth that mattered was this: Laura Salinas was now free and she was now his.

Antonio Vázquez was left there under the trees, face down, his hands open and his eyes crushed; he was left there, inert, stretched out near the statue of the goddess, who must have been Diana given that she carried bow, arrows and quiver. Diana was the daughter of Zeus, sister of Apollo, Lady of the Chase and of Hunting, and immune to desire. It is said that the inhabitants of Tauris would sacrifice in her honour any shipwrecked sailor that the sea cast up on their island shores.

22

A New Life

On 30 July, Alcaén left the insurance company at about
seven o'clock, stopped by his apartment to change, threw
a box full of old clothes into a skip and went off to the
Bar Vizcaya to meet Laura, as they had agreed before the
crime. It meant, therefore, they had not seen each other
for just over a month, a period which for him had fallen
into two opposing halves: on the one hand, there was the
fear, an atrocious, indelible fear that caused Alcaén to
wake terrified in the middle of the night, in shivers, or
sent him down every morning, his legs trembling uncontrollably, to the newsstand, to sit and read the paper with
his heart pounding against him like a workman's mallet
against the sides of an empty house, a heavy mallet
demolishing walls, busting down partitions, reducing it
all until it was small enough to fit into the word destruction or into the word oblivion. Up until then, Alcaén's
crime had yet to be resolved, the police were analysing
the fingerprints found on the murder weapon, trying to
gather statements. The newspapers, for the time being,
were making no mention of Laura Salinas nor had they
given the crime much coverage, barely a column on the
front page, and, later on, a couple of brief items: the murder of the lottery ticket seller remains unsolved, no
motive is apparent; that it may have been a settling of

scores or a case of mistaken identity has not been ruled out. And, after that, they stopped writing about Antonio Vázquez. The case was put on file, another one of the many that go unpunished every year.

The second half of Alcaén's existence had no relation to fear, on the contrary: he felt radiant, happy, optimistic. He had just painted his apartment, the walls a pale ochre (to go with Laura's eyes), the ceilings white. He had put a couple of display cabinets for books in the living room and also renewed a large part of his furnishings; he had various designer polo shirts and three new suits in his wardrobe, and fifty per cent of his chest of drawers was full of underwear as yet unworn. The other fifty per cent was empty, awaiting Laura Salinas's things, since this was what they had decided when the two of them put together the plan to eliminate Antonio Vázquez: that she would sell that devil's abode, that horrific prison hidden away inside an innocent-seeming apartment block. In two or three years' time they would sell his home too, and with the sum total of the two transactions, plus their two salaries, they'd be able to afford a house with a garden, a residence of the kind he had so desired. Could a person ask for more? He already had the princess he'd always dreamed of and, very soon, he would have the palace.

Alcaén threw away several hard-core videos and magazines, crossed out the number of a brothel he had been to from time to time, and from where, on certain solitary nights, girls had been dispatched to his apartment. Some of them he remembered: young women who were beautiful or plain, Spanish or South-American, white or black, and who at first, as they counted his money or dealt with his credit card, kept themselves out of range, unpursuable, sheltering behind an easygoing professionalism, a preventive composure. 'Would you mind signing here?' they'd say, in a clinical, distant voice. 'Could I see some form of ID, your national identity card or your passport?' But immediately afterwards, the formalities concluded, their voice and attitude would change, they'd lay an expert hand over his groin, caress it, lower a zip or undo a button with hot, uninhibited fingers, saying, 'What do you like, sweetheart, what turns you on?' Alcaén shook his head to drive that sordidness away; wanting it out of his life for ever.

Instead of all that, Alcaén dedicated those four long weeks to reading. He had bought a whole stack of books, some recent publications and some classic works of the sort Iker Orbáiz and Ángel Biedma would often discuss; he had read them voraciously and placed them inside his display cabinets. He couldn't wait to talk about them with Laura. He couldn't wait for her to come and occupy the centre of his new life.

Naturally, he had felt the temptation to call her on more than one occasion, in the course of those interminable forty days and forty nights. But he hadn't, in part to prove to her his resolve and in part because they were both sure that the police would have tapped the phone line of the widow – as Laura had called herself on the afternoon they plotted her husband's murder, perhaps already with a certain malice, savouring her freedom.

Now, at last, they were going to meet again. Everything was settled, the danger had passed. One of these evenings he'd take her with him to the Sívori and she would dazzle his friends. He'd return with Laura, heaped in glory, like a king returning to his country from a long exile, sailing into port to reclaim his throne; for during his self-imposed quarantine, spent reading and doing up his home, he had been fearful, for whatever reason, of arousing any suspicions, and so he had reduced the frequency of his trips to Gloria's bar; when there, he had not said another word to Ángel and Iker about Laura Salinas – not that they had asked about her again, because they were still obsessed with the novel and nothing else mattered to them. Alcaén wasn't put out by this; on the contrary, inwardly he congratulated himself on his discretion and ingenuity. If that pompous Ángel Biedma only knew who he really was and what he had done!

And, anyway, what point did any of that have? None, no point at all, he told himself, as he passed the doorway where he had kissed Laura Salinas, where she had bitten his lips, where he had fondled her heavenly breasts; what point did anything have at that precise moment, now that he could already make out, fifty, sixty metres away, the sign that read Bar Vizcaya and, by extension, the start of his beautiful future.

He took out the packet of thin black cigarillos, which now truly belonged to him, and lit one. And then he remembered the sheets – the other item he'd bought along with the books, the polo shirts, the display cabinets and the suits: sheets, exquisite satin sheets, green, purple, blue; fine sheets that would become Laura Salinas's natural habitat, the logical complement to her naked body.

He entered the Bar Vizcaya ten minutes early. It was Friday afternoon, and so the place was crowded. He went through to the rear, to the spot where they had been the last time, and he tried to find the posture in which he wanted her to see him when she arrived: hand in pocket, both hands on the bar, standing up, sitting on a bar stool, with his back to her and in profile, his elbows on the bar . . . He selected one of these postures, ordered a bottle of beer and settled down to wait.

Which he did; he waited and waited, one hour, two hours, two and a half. He waited until no one else was left. He waited until the bar closed, until there could be no question that Laura Salinas, for whatever reason, was not going to come.

23

Everyone Lies

It was not hard for him to persuade Iker Orbáiz to go and see Laura Salinas, but neither had it been easy to arrive at that idea, which struck him suddenly, just when he was at his most bewildered by the pain and exhaustion, at the moment when he had thought all was irretrievably lost; and then it happened: there Iker was, right next to him, it was like bumping into someone in the dark. Iker Orbáiz: he would definitely be a good messenger.

But before he reached that solution, and after two days of unconditional insomnia – the Friday and the Saturday, during which he'd been unable to sleep for a single second – Alcaén had considered the matter from all possible (as well as impossible) angles, and he had come up with so many reasonable as well as crazy explanations, so many ominous questions and harmful answers that there came a point on his descent into hell when he seriously believed that he would lose his mind.

Best of all his conclusions was that Laura had been unable to come because of some trivial problem or, simply, because she'd been afraid to, had had a bad feeling; or because she'd found out she was still under surveillance and hadn't wanted to compromise him. As for his worst conjectures, they were awful, two of them in particular: in the first scenario, something serious had happened to her, she was in hospital, ill, perhaps badly injured, in intensive care, or else under arrest in a cell, held in a prison, taking all the blame for the murder out of loyalty to him, so as not to incriminate him; in the second, Laura had obviously deceived him; she had seduced him and used him to rid her of Antonio Vázquez and now never wanted to see him again, now that she was out of danger, perhaps in the company of another man. A fatalist by nature, Alcaén Sánchez took this possibility almost for granted; in fact, of all the versions of the woman he'd imagined in the course of that torment – Laura in a green hospital gown, Laura in prisoner's uniform – this was by far the one that recurred most often: he saw her standing in a doorway with that other man, guiding his hand to her breasts, biting his lips; or, refining the scene now with a morbid persistence, on his bed naked, cavorting on his dirty sheets, suddenly transformed into a coarse, vulgar creature, like on the day he'd told her about his plan to rob the insurance company, perhaps laughing about him: Can you believe it? He bumped that bastard off with a monkey wrench, he was drooling for me, the creep, I can't tell you how revolting he was, I wouldn't fuck him even if I was lent another cunt, I didn't give him anything in return, know what I mean, the odd kiss here, a bit of a fondle there, and 'that's all you're getting, that's as far as we go', the stupid jerk . . . Alcaén knew that this was ridiculous, inconceivable; he knew he was raving, but even so, he couldn't stop torturing himself.

Early on Saturday morning, a wreck from anxiety and lack of sleep, he went back to the Bar Vizcaya, where he took up his position in the usual spot, ordered a breakfast he hardly touched and some lunch, three hours later; but Laura didn't show. And that night, he did the same again, he went to the bar in search of a miracle, ordered something to eat, a beer, and afterwards two more; he waited in vain. All of a sudden, he felt certain that the girl was dead. But was that how *he* wanted to be, he wondered.

What could he do? To call her at work on Monday was very risky, she'd warned him never to do that, whatever happened, for the estate agency would in all likelihood be under surveillance, the phone lines tapped. To go to her house was even worse, it'd be the equivalent of giving them both away, to putting themselves in the spotlight. Worst of all was to return to the scene of the crime, he told himself, criminals always do that and they're always caught.

And it was just as he was thinking this that the idea came to him to use Iker Orbáiz. Wasn't Iker in the habit of visiting certain places where a crime had been committed and of collecting information, impressions, signs of the tragedy? Didn't he describe this as fieldwork, a fact-finding mission? Alcaén needed to get Iker to see Laura Salinas. And he needed him to do it without taking any unnecessary risks. He wasn't sure it was much of a plan, but he didn't have a better one.

He left the Bar Vizcaya and went directly to the Sívori. He took a taxi, lit a cigarillo, ran a feverish hand over his cheeks and chin; from the rough feel of his face, he supposed he must have looked in a pitiful state: unshaven, unwashed, circles under his sunken eyes, the features of a wolf-man. But he couldn't go to his apartment to freshen up, it was very late, he thought that Iker and Ángel might already have left; he cursed himself for his stupidity and stubbornness, for his slow reflexes, for how long it had taken him to form this strategy. There was no cause for all that neurosis, though: when he arrived, his friends were still there.

'How are you, Alcaén?' Iker greeted him. 'Hey, are you all right? You don't look so well.'

Ángel Biedma greeted him with a brief hand gesture, and watched him suspiciously.

'Yeah, I, um . . . think I've caught the flu . . . or something, don't know what. Didn't sleep well last night. Anyway, how's the novel getting on? Have you finished it?'

'Not yet. By the way, that reminds me, I wanted to ask you a favour.'

'Anything you like.'

'With your permission, what you told me about the false adverts, the ones about the houses, would come in handy. Using it in the novel, I mean.'

Alcaén glanced at Ángel.

'Well . . . it's a bit embarrassing, but as far as I'm concerned, if it's of use to you . . .'

'I appreciate it. It could turn out to be good material, you never know.'

Again, Alcaén rubbed his hand over his chin.

'Look, um, now you mention it . . . about looking for material . . . I was wondering if you'd heard about that unsolved crime, a man called . . . Velázquez, I think it was, or Vázquez, Antonio Vázquez or something like that. He was done in about a month ago, in a park near his home. Ring a bell?'

'No, actually it doesn't. What's so interesting about it?'

'Yeah, right,' Ángel cut in, rather ill-temperedly, 'what makes you so interested in that story. Is it perhaps something . . . personal?'

Alcaén sensed that clear-eyed, predatory stare close in. He felt a rise of fear.

'No, nothing in particular. Well . . . it's just that I may have known the man . . . the victim. Or rather, no not him, his wife.'

'Really?' Ángel Biedma inquired. 'And where did you know her from?'

Alcaén looked at him and knew at once that he was being studied. Ángel's eyes seemed to bore into him – as furiously as an animal scratching out another's den.

'Oh, it's a . . . how shall I put it? . . . very long story. Actually, I'd almost rather not tell it to you. Don't know why I said anything, it's probably nothing important. Unless the victim is the person I'm thinking of . . . I can't quite remember if the newspaper mentioned Vázquez or Velázquez. But the area was the same, he lived around there. Anyway, I thought: as Iker's interested in these things, he might want to go and take a look. I just need to give him the address, that's all.'

'And what would I find there?'

'Ah, that I don't know, that's for you to find out. You could talk to the neighbours, and if it's the person I'm thinking of, I'll tell you about him. Or to his wife. You could also talk to his wife. You know, get the details first-hand. You might even get a surprise; like I said, I'll tell you about it afterwards.'

Was he aware that he was playing with fire? Yes, he was. What else could he have done? Wait for Laura Salinas's phone call? And if there was no phone call? He needed to know something, anything; nothing could be worse than all that anxiety, that helplessness. Maybe Iker would find her or maybe not; maybe she no longer lived there. Alcaén was prepared for that too. He was prepared for a lot of things, but not for the truth.

'All right,' Iker Orbáiz said, 'why not? After all, you're one of my suppliers, you've just given me your story about the adverts. And you also told me about robbing your company.'

'Right; but that you can't publish.'

'I know. Don't worry.'

'That'd be too compromising. Someone might read the book and then steal the money,' said Ángel, and in his hand the word money took on the shape of a tarantula.

Alcaén got up. His eyes stung. He barely had the strength to leave.

'I'm going to go and lie down,' he said, unable to stifle a yawn. 'This flu . . . I feel shattered. Maybe I'll see you tomorrow. If in the end you go to where I said . . .'

'Tomorrow,' Iker interrupted. 'Tomorrow – seeing as it's Sunday – I'll go and check out your dead guy.'

Ángel Biedma's eyes followed Alcaén right to the door. Alcaén could feel them fixed on his back, eagle-eyes, scorpion-eyes, hook-eyes; he could feel them behind him, suspecting him, pestering; they came in to his home, hornet-eyes, crab-eyes, they observed him fall exhausted, still dressed, onto his incongruous satin sheets.

But they were gone by the time he woke up, when the telephone rang and, incredibly, it was six in the afternoon, he'd slept fifteen hours, and on lifting the receiver he heard Iker Orbáiz' voice telling him, You've got it wrong, that man wasn't who you thought he was; Iker told him this straight out, without preamble or background music, with the raw suddenness with which these things happen in real life, without beating about the bush with phrases that were unfinished or confused or badly punctuated; he told him this: You've got it wrong, that man wasn't who you thought he was, Antonio Vázquez, it must be someone else, his neighbours don't know anything, he worked in the centre, selling lottery tickets, he was a loner.

'But what about his wife? Didn't you see her?'

'Well,' Iker Orbáiz replied, 'that's just it, that's how I know you've got the wrong guy: Antonio Vázquez wasn't married.'

24

This is Just the Beginning

Here is where this story begins. Here is where one of us three, exactly as I told you at the start, sets out from his home, at about eleven-thirty at night, to go and kill Laura Salinas. By now, of course, you'll know who that devastated man is, that man with no way out who walks with slow, unsteady steps through a city where a storm has just raged and whose eyes have a fevered, shattered look; you'll know that he is not in fact someone dangerous, but someone frightened, and that as he advances towards his crime he is afraid of the darkened parks and the silent streets, disquieted by the lines of motionless cars, of the dogs that don't bark, the people you can't see, the locked-up shops; you'll know that he is thinking about the day he killed Antonio Vázquez, going over and over a thousand times each of the things he did, wondering if he might have left behind something that could give him away, any small clue; wondering too if his pain will ever end, that sharp, all-encompassing pain, that slow, sinuous snake of pain; if it will disappear from him bit by bit, if in time it will fade, just like when the snow melts, the wolf tracks do too. You all know that this man is Alcaén Sánchez and why he wants to murder Laura Salinas.

However, all that came later; it started, as I already told you, at eleven-thirty that very night. Five or so hours earlier, when he put the phone down on Iker Orbáiz, Alcaén experienced an inexplicable sense of well-being, an almost physical relief, as if he had just let something heavy drop from his hands. Then came the questions, and with them the fear. Who had he killed when he killed Antonio Vázquez? Where did that leave him – that crime that was no longer an act of justice, a logical, irreproachable action, like shooting vermin or crushing an insect? Who was Laura Salinas and why had she deceived him? He floundered about in that swamp for hours, and got nowhere.

He remembered the man he had murdered, how he had searched his face for the marks of evil, the telltale signs of the monster. He saw again his sallow complexion, his greasy hair, his dirty, saffron-coloured teeth, and no longer did these add up to an abject, repulsive creature, only to an ordinary man, an innocent. In parallel with this, even as Alcaén restored and absolved Antonio Vázquez, he was distilling an immense hatred for Laura Salinas, a hatred that was tragic, implacable, like the pounding of waves against rocks, full of rancour and a desire for revenge. He felt so stupid in that recently painted apartment, with its purple sheets and brand-new clothes! Who was Laura Salinas? Why had she turned him into a lunatic, a murderer? For hours he struggled in those dark, infinite waters. In the street a summer storm broke, the rain poured down, then suddenly ceased, leaving behind in the city a smell of rotting flowers, an odour of destruction and of oblivion.

At eleven-thirty he left his apartment. He stopped a taxi and went to the area where Antonio Vázquez had lived; he went to the railway station, to the modest public gardens where he had killed him at the foot of some trees, near a statue of the goddess Diana. Then he went as far as the man's home; he looked at the red-brick building where Laura Salinas had certainly never lived, where she had never been woken in the middle of the night, never been slapped or had her fingers broken, where no one had ever said to her, On your knees, bitch, scream and I'll kill you. What had happened exactly? Why had she made him kill Antonio Vázquez?

Alcaén went to a couple of places and had a couple of drinks. Then he flagged down another taxi, went to the house in the private development where he'd first met Laura Salinas, where he'd imagined a life at her side. The windows were dark, but there was a light on in the porch – a light diffused by several objects left lying around outside, two cups, a tricycle, some rackets no doubt somewhat damaged as a result of the rain. For a few minutes he stayed there, faced with these signs of other people's happiness, breathing in the fragrant air of the gardens, that spiced air composed of the scent of pine trees and plants, of rose bushes and swimming pools.

Back in the city, he had another couple of drinks, went to the brothel whose number he'd crossed out in his address book, drank more alcohol, spoke to someone in an office, was asked for his national identity card, took out his credit card, a girl said to him, What do you like, big boy, what turns you on, stroking his cheeks, his chin, and, as she did so, Alcaén could hear in the palms of her hands his maniac's stubble, his wolf-man's face.

At some point it was Monday already. At seven in the morning he left the club, only to find himself in an incomprehensible world devoid of Latin music, Caribbean women, orange-painted walls. He went to more places and had more drinks, a coffee.

At half past eight he stationed himself near Laura Salinas' estate agency. At nine, the staff began to arrive, but none of them were her. At ten, without stopping by his home, he headed off to his insurance company. What were they going to think of him, how could he turn up late for work, unshaven, dirty, his shirt covered in stains. He'd think of an excuse, he told himself, and told himself the same thing again as he neared his office and spotted Señor Montero waiting for him at the main entrance, there perhaps to demand an explanation in private, to avoid a scene. As Alcaén approached he recognised Señor Montero only gradually, as the eyes, hands, implacable baldness and sharp, severe profile came into focus.

But he was unable to recognise the two men on either side of Señor Montero, the ones who came up to him when he arrived, took hold of his arms, said, Are you Alcaén Sánchez?, come with us to the station, in accordance with Article 520 of the Criminal Code you have the right to remain silent, you have the right to appoint a lawyer or to ask for one to be appointed on your behalf, you have the right to make a telephone call to a member of your family or to a person of your choice. In their abstract voices they said, 'You are under arrest for the murder of Antonio Vázquez.'

25

Six Letters

He had his photograph taken in a lab, his fingerprints taken on a counter and a blood sample drawn in the infirmary. His blood was Rh-negative, and his fingerprints, plain arch. Next, he was taken to an office, and there an officer and a typist took a statement from him. After that, he was transferred to a room in which there were two inspectors, one thin the other fat, one dressed in a blue suit the other, grey. It was a tiny room with dim light and poor ventilation; it hardly had any furniture, save for a table, two chairs and several filing cabinets. They're going to beat me up, was Alcaén's first thought. I've heard they make you wear a wetsuit and hit you with rubber tubes; they know how to break your bones without leaving marks; they put you in freezing water and then in boiling water; they pull your nails out with pliers, throw you down stairs. On the table was an ashtray, a tape-recorder that was running, a paperweight.

'Have a seat,' said the thin police officer, gesturing courteously to one of the chairs and then sitting down in the one opposite him.

'I'm Captain Urzáiz and this is Sergeant Gelman.'

He stared at Alcaén, as if expecting him to do something. Alcaén did nothing, except to stare back at the police officer, at his long dark hands, black eyes, his arid-looking skin, almost an imitation skin, synthetic, ruined perhaps by lack of sunlight and dirty work.

The fat man was not simply fat, he was much more than that: he had an enormous head, a face disfigured by flab and a stomach around which a cycle tour could have been staged. His sole remaining trace of humanity was a pair of shrewd, sharp eyes, of a blue light enough to produce in the person they regarded a sensation of coldness. The rest of him produced precisely the opposite impression: stifling heat and exhaustion. And it was this ninety per cent that picked up Alcaén's statement, gave it a cursory glance and threw it disdainfully back down on the table. He then gave Alcaén a hostile smile, full of scorn, a smile liable to stop a buffalo herd in its tracks.

'Why did you kill Antonio Vázquez? You don't explain that in there,' he said, pointing at the statement.

'I don't know who Antonio Vázquez is. I don't know what you're talking about or why I'm here. I intend to file a formal complaint as soon as . . .'

'You think I won't give you a good slap?' the fat man yelled, and started towards Alcaén. But Captain Urzáiz raised his hand.

'Gelman, for God's sake. Calm down. Let's hear what the man has to say.'

'But are we going to let this scum threaten us? I asked you a question. Why did you kill the lottery ticket seller? Did you owe him money or what? Were you trying to rob him? Were you lovers? Whose prints are those on the wrench you struck him with on the back of the neck?

Those of a friend, those of the checkout operator in the place where you bought it?'

On the outside, Alcaén folded his arms in a show of the serenity he did not feel. What was going on on the inside can be summed up in two words: gnawing anxiety.

'You've made a mistake; you've got the wrong man. I haven't killed anyone. What prints are you talking about?' He felt strengthened as he said this, remembering they'd have no proof against him, it was impossible. They've got nothing, he told himself, there're no witnesses, there're no clues. Who or what, then, had led them to him? For the time being that wasn't important; when you feel trapped it doesn't matter who's after you, only how you're going to escape.

'What prints am I talking about? You know exactly which ones,' said Gelman defiantly.

'No I don't know. I don't know anything about any murdered man or any monkey wrench. You've got it wrong, Captain. This must all be a misunderstanding.'

Urzáiz and Gelman exchanged a glance.

'All right, all right, let's see now,' intervened Urzáiz, his voice armed with patience, as if he were a teacher trying to drum a lesson home to his pupils. He then took out a packet of Ducados and offered one to Alcaén. 'Hot in here, isn't it? Like an oven. You smoke?'

'Not now, thank you.'

'But you do smoke, don't you? Thin black cigarillos.'

Alcaén's chin began to tremble. He passed a hand over it in an attempt to stop the trembling, a calming hand, like that of a man attempting to tame an animal by stroking it – and he remembered his dishevelled appearance, the villain's stubble, the vulpine features, the swindler's circles under the eyes.

'Yes, sometimes.'

There was a knock on the door and a uniformed police officer came in and handed a sheet of paper to Sergeant Gelman who, after looking at it, gave it to the Captain.

'Well, well,' Urzáiz went on, 'sometimes, you say. The fact is, that day you were smoking.'

'What day?'

'The day you killed the lottery ticket seller, for fuck's sake!' Gelman shouted. 'June the twenty-first – or has it already slipped your mind?'

Alcaén almost felt like laughing out loud. Just how far did they expect to get with those cheap tricks? Of course he hadn't been smoking when he killed Antonio Vázquez. They haven't got anything on me, he thought, they haven't got anything at all.

'June the twenty-first?' he said. 'You want me to remember if I was or wasn't smoking on June the twenty-first?'

'Listen, my friend,' Urzáiz's tone became more familiar as his voice dropped to a near whisper, 'it so happens that we found a butt from a cigarillo next to the body. And the saliva on it is yours. It'll be very easy to prove that it's yours. DNA testing – it never lies.'

'That's impossible, that's . . .!'

'And poor Antonio Vázquez must have put up a fight, eh?' said Sergeant Gelman, leaning against the filing cabinets and now strangely calm. 'Meaning it couldn't have been easy for you. His shirt was ripped, so he must have punched you, right? Was it a punch or a kick? Or did you cause your own injury?'

'What injury? I have no idea what you're trying to get at, Sergeant, but I can assure you . . .'

'And then you cleaned the blood off and lost the handkerchief. Or maybe he grabbed it from you, because it was under his arm. They do that sometimes, they grab one last thing before they fall, as if trying to hold onto this world. Admit it! You're trapped.'

'Handkerchief? What handkerchief? You're making the whole thing up, both of you!'

'I'm afraid not, my friend,' Urzáiz continued, in his professorial style. 'There was a handkerchief under the body of Antonio Vázquez. A bloodstained handkerchief. It's your blood, my friend, Rh-negative, the same blood you supplied us with just now in the infirmary. And blood never lies, son, it can't be altered, it can't be faked. Blood has its own arithmetic, its own laws; it's the world of plasma and red blood cells, leucocytes and lymphocytes, oxygen and carbon dioxide. If we've got your blood, we've got you.'

That was the moment when Alcaén Sánchez understood. It came in a flash, the images flicking through his mind in a few seconds, causing him a sense of a disbelief and pain, like when you cut yourself with a knife. Urzáiz was right – it was his blood, the blood that Laura Salinas had stolen from him. He remembered the evening they had run out of the Bar Vizcaya, he remembered when they stepped into the doorway and she had opened her coat, taking hold of his hand and bringing it up to her breasts, her wonderful, heavenly breasts, kissed him with such sweet savagery, with thirsty desire, biting his lips desperately, until he bled. And then she had pulled away, dabbed a handkerchief to her lips, and, staring at that vis- cous, scarlet liquid she had said: 'If only that were true, my God, if only he were dead!'

Gelman was right – he was trapped. Laura had trapped him with his own plan to rob the insurance company! It was almost all there: there was the cigarette butt, which she must have picked up on any one of the occasions they'd been together; there was the false blood, as false as the blood he had taken from the toilet in the Sívori, only this blood as well as being false was also genuine . . . The room began to pitch, as though he were seeing it from the cabin of a ship. All was clear now, Laura Salinas had made him kill Antonio Vázquez and then she had left the false clues by the body. But why?

The door of the office opened, in came two policemen; Gelman told them:

'Take him down to the cells.'

'Wait a moment!' Alcaén shouted. 'Did you say June the twenty-first? Now that I think about it, that evening I stayed at home. In the morning I went to the office and in the evening I was watching television. I remember a friend called me. Talk to him, his name is Ángel Biedma. Afterwards we met up in a bar called the Sívori. Speak to all these people: speak to my colleagues at work, to Doctor Biedma, to the people who were in the bar.'

'We already have,' Sergeant Gelman said. 'And you're

right, you were at the office and at the bar. And in between you killed that man, you killed him like a dog. Why, Alcaén? What was the reason?'

The two policemen took hold of his arms.

'Call Ángel Biedma! He'll tell you that he was talking with me.'

'My friend, we've done that,' Captain Urzáiz said. 'Actually, he's the one who led us to you. Without meaning to; quite by chance. I bet you'd like to know how. I'll tell you: he asked a patient of his who's an officer on the force if he knew anything about Antonio Vázquez; he told him a friend had mentioned the crime to him the night before, that this friend had been very interested, that he even sent someone to the dead man's home to investigate. The inspector looked into the case, called back the next day and asked Doctor Biedma two questions: if his friend smoked and what brand. And Biedma answered that he did and that it was some brand of thin black cigarillos. So you see, you were unlucky, the doctor wanted to help you, only he did the exact opposite.'

'I have the right to call a lawyer,' said Alcaén, as they lifted him to his feet. 'You've got no proof against me. Anyone could have left that handkerchief and cigarette butt next to the body. You're making a mistake.'

'Of course you can call a lawyer, my friend,' Urzáiz concluded. 'Who's stopping you? In this country, everyone has that right – even a scum like you.'

Alcaén was being led out, head bowed, handcuffed, when Sergeant Gelman, with a big smile on his massive face, said:

'Oh, by the way! At the trial you'll also have to explain how you knew that Antonio Vázquez was killed with a monkey wrench.'

'You said so.'

'Come on, mate – I didn't tell you that. It's all there, recorded on tape. That way you can listen to it whenever you like. I told you it'd been done with a wrench, but not that it'd been done with a monkey wrench. Nice little trick, wasn't it?'

'Monkey,' Alcaén Sánchez repeated to himself, 'a monkey wrench.' No doubt in years to come he would often think about the word that had been his downfall. 'Monkey,' he'd tell himself; 'it's a word in the singular, it has three vowels, three consonants, and two syllables, with the stress on the first; it's a six-letter word, like killer, like deceit, like prison.'

He entered his cell. Let himself drop onto the bed. He fell asleep remembering Laura Salinas: it had been so beautiful when she began to descend over his life like snow over a small darkened city. He saw her perfect lips, her hands, her ochre eyes – eyes that were feline, sandy, reminiscent of a plant that concealed in the earth a great root. Snow falls and transforms everything, making it clean, magical; walk on it and you're in the sky, touch it with your fingers and you're a child for ever. But in truth it is nothing, it changes nothing; when it melts the dirty roads reappear, the dreary streets, the withered trees. The snow fades without a trace, vanishes without a sound. The snow is silent.

26

The Dark Zone

Iker Orbáiz shook Sergeant Gelman's hand and walked off down the corridors of the police station. Under normal circumstances, he would have spotted several detectives with fierce eyes and stubborn jawlines, a woman in tears by the drinks machine; the clichéd mannerisms of three or four kings of the underworld, who were moving to and fro in a whole series of invertebrate swingings and swayings, bobbing about as though made of cork and subject to currents. But that morning Iker noticed none of these things. That morning all he could think of was Alcaén Sánchez and his terrible story.

He had visited Alcaén a couple of times in prison; his heart had sunk on seeing the ravages of prison on the young man's face, on seeing the pointed nose, the shaved hair, the extinguished eyes; nor could he forget, of course, the story that Alcaén had told him and that you all already know. Alcaén had reminded Iker of what he knew before – his meeting Laura Salinas through the estate agency, his pretending to be a big shot, his honesty in telling her about his plan to rob the insurance company, and how this honesty had been his downfall. But Alcaén had also told him the darkest part, all the deeds and lies that had led to that terrible abyss, to that ever-descending spiral of traps, betrayals and crimes.

'Well, Iker,' he had said to him with dreadful sadness, as they said goodbye, with a sadness that took in his lips, his forehead, his gaze, that took in all of him, 'didn't you want my life to make a book? Here it is; help yourself to whatever you like.'

Iker could not forget Alcaén's expression as he had said this; he could not forget those words, that bankrupt face, that look of a man about to step off a cliff, to go under, to say farewell to everything.

He went to the hospital where Ángel Biedma worked. He'd phoned him to arrange eating together, and, on entering the clinic's restaurant, he caught sight of him at the back, oblivious to those around him, to the din of the conversations and the concave sound of spoons, sitting in exactly the same place he always sat, his statuesque hands motionless on the table, on either side of the plate, the cutlery meticulously arranged, the water glass just over half full and which he kept filling to maintain at this level.

'Iker, my dear,' said Dr Biedma, raising both hands by way of welcome.

'How are you, Ángel?'

'Glad you've come. Everything going well? Have you finished the novel? You didn't have much left to go.'

'Not so well, to tell you the truth. I'm worried about Alcaén. I went to see him again in prison today. It scares me to think that that's where he's going to end his days, to think he's been sentenced to thirty-five years.'

'Don't you believe it. Nowadays they let them out quickly, they don't have room for them all. He'll be there ten years, max.'

'Max?'

'I mean, ten is twenty-five less than thirty-five. A pretty good reduction.'

'I've also been to the police station, to see Sergeant Gelman. An intelligent man.'

'That slob . . . Oh well, if you felt like seeing something horrible before lunch, you made the perfect choice. But tell me, what's poor old Alcaén Sánchez saying these days. Have you told him you're going to use his story in your novel? Because I suppose you will now, won't you? Who'd pass up that kind of material! A mine, Iker: all you need to do is dig and the gold is yours. I really must congratulate you.'

'Yes, maybe. Anyway, this whole business is strange.'

'Not strange, Iker: it's sordid, horrible. Alcaén murdered a man in cold blood. A man he'd never spoken to before.'

'But what I don't understand is the role of Laura Salinas. Gelman tells me they've conducted an in-depth investigation and there's not the slightest doubt about her relationship with Antonio Vázquez: there was none; she, too, had never set eyes on him.'

'Yeah, you already told me Alcaén's version. But don't you think he's making it up? He killed Vázquez, he's confessed to it. According to him, he killed him because this Laura Salinas talked him into it.'

'And who talked her into it? That's the crucial part of the story. Why did she force him to commit a crime from which she had nothing to gain?'

'Well . . .' pondering his reply, Ángel Biedma stared down at his hands, at that moment immobile but transformed at once, as he set out his theories, into dagger hands '. . . two answers come to mind: one that Alcaén is insane, and the other that he did it to harm the girl. She, as you yourself told me, declared that Alcaén never left her alone; her colleagues at work have confirmed that he used to call her constantly, to the point that she had to hand in her notice in order to escape from him.'

'Alcaén says that's not true.'

'That she didn't leave her job or that he didn't pursue her?'

'He didn't pursue her and you know it. He gave up on her after he told her that he wasn't a millionaire, that he wasn't going to buy that luxury home or do anything of the sort. She was furious about his lying, and so he forgot about her. Remember, he told us that one evening in the Sívori. He even told us, laughing at himself, about his plan to rob the insurance company and get the money.'

'Why did he go back to her, then, if you say that he had given up on her?'

'She called him. Soon after that conversation in the Sívori she called him at his office and told him the story about her cruel husband, she stole Alcaén's blood, told him . . .'

'Whoa, just a moment! He says she did all this, but that's not true. It's an incredible story and out of it you'll make an even more incredible novel. But, my dear, I fear it's not real. Reality is never so perfect.'

'That's what I think. By the way: Alcaén told me that that business about adverts for non-existent houses was your idea, that he did it because you'd asked him to, so that I'd have something to put in my novel.'

Ángel looked annoyed.

'So he told you . . .'

'Actually I guessed as much from something he said. Then I wormed it out of him. "Didn't you want my life for a book?"'

'And?'

'I told him that we'd talked about using aspects of him to construct a character. That he was going to be a sort of model. And he told me that you asked him to do the adverts. That you were both in the Sívori and that you started telling him about a painting.'

'By Goya,' Ángel Biedma interrupted. 'A Goya painting, Saturn devouring his son.'

'But that didn't seem enough for you, did it?' – the tone of Iker's voice had suddenly hardened. Dr Biedma's hands came to rest once more on the tablecloth.

'Now you've lost me. I don't follow.'

'Really? My novel wasn't progressing because Alcaén's life was too ordinary, just like everyone's. So you decided to change it a little. Isn't that right?'

'Iker, I think you've been spending too much time with that obese policeman. I think the most sensible . . .'

'Shut up!' Iker slammed his fist down on the table. The other customers in the restaurant turned to look at them. Ángel Biedma's cutlery jumbled; a spoon fell to the floor.

'Look, kiddo, I won't tolerate you shouting at me.'

'Oh, I think you will. You'll tolerate that and a whole lot more.'

'As long you stop going on about that absurd story.'

'It's not an absurd story, it's the truth. It was you who called Laura Salinas after what Alcaén told us in the Sívori. It was you who came up with that whole story about the brutal husband. You wanted to know how far a man like Alcaén would go. You started with the adverts and then you got the idea of hiring Laura Salinas. You chose a victim at random, that's why no link could be established between her and the false husband. You chose poor Antonio Vázquez, but it could have been anyone else.'

'Well, if all that were true, it would suggest you mean a great deal to me.'

'How much did you pay her, Ángel? I suppose her price was very high.'

Dr Biedma smiled.

'Good things have a high price, you know that.'

'You thought the police would catch him very quickly and that I'd get my story; and to make sure he didn't get away with it you took his ideas for robbing the insurance company, the saliva on the cigarette, the false blood. Only Alcaén turned out to be twice as smart as you had expected, and he did the job without leaving any clues. So you put in action your plan B, or maybe you'd had that ready from the start: you gave him away to one of your patients, a police inspector. Then, when they questioned you, you ruined his alibi, saying you didn't remember having called him that night, denying him the only chance he had. But you did call him, and that'll be easy to prove, I can assure you.'

'Oh really? How?'

'The police know. He told you to phone him at the precise time you knew he was going to kill Antonio Vázquez and you did, so as not to alarm him, but from a telephone box so your number wouldn't be registered. Sergeant Gelman's checked that there was a call to Alcaén's mobile at the time you arranged, made from a public telephone.'

'In which case that's all they know: that he received a call from a phone box, but not who from.'

'It was you, Ángel. And the fact that it was you and that you've denied it proves that it was also you who thought up the rest of the story.'

Ángel gave another laugh, satisfied.

'Well, Iker, you won't deny at least that it makes a great story. Aren't you proud of me? It's yours. You know how I've always liked giving you presents.'

The doctor then turned his attention to the food and opened the menu like a monster opening its third eye.

'Yes,' Iker said. 'That's true. Do you remember what the first one was?'

'The first present I gave you?'

'That's right. Do you remember it?'

'Absolutely: it was a miniature tape recorder. A sophisticated little gadget, Japanese.'

'Exactly – the cassette-recorder that's in my pocket and on which I've just recorded this whole conversation.' Iker Orbáiz sat back his chair and smiled. 'Ángel, my dear, how come you didn't think I'd pull a stunt as obvious as that.'

For a few seconds Dr Biedma observed him, his face distorted with rage. Then he smiled again. A baleful, twisted smile.

'It won't be much use to you,' he said. 'I'm not a nobody like your Alcaén Sánchez. I'm not short of resources.'

'We'll see about that. We'll see what happens when Laura Salinas cracks.'

'Nothing will happen to me,' said Ángel Biedma. 'It's hard for them to catch you if you hide behind your money.'

27

This Side of the Devil

He was right in part, but not completely. The judge in charge of our case accepted Iker's cassette as evidence, and Laura Salinas, a woman of few scruples and even less character, broke down the moment Sergeant Gelman got his hands on her. They sentenced me to eleven years, although I doubt I'll serve more than three, and I'm sure that anyone who wasn't me would have got at least fifteen. I'm not complaining. Nor will I hide from you – because I already told you this earlier – that at first I suffered a great deal; as you can guess, a prison is hardly the best place for a man of my taste and position. But I have been here now for precisely six hundred and twenty-three days, not one more not one less; I've learnt to put a brave face on things – hard bread needs sharp teeth, and all that – and I am rather proud of my ability to camouflage myself among the riffraff they've got locked up in here; you can't begin to imagine what this is like, what sort of trash collects in a hole like this. But that's OK – I am, above all, an essentially chameleonic being, and whilst that might not make me any stronger, it does make me harder to catch. Do you like chameleons? Me, I adore them; to me they don't seem fickle creatures, as they do to many people, but clever and beautiful. In fact, I have a photograph of one right here, pinned to the wall. As you well know, it can change the colour of its skin in order to adapt to its surroundings. It has a whole range of greens, yellows, reds and ochres that appear and fade according to light stimulation from its immediate environment; its legs and tail are prehensile and, best of all perhaps, its eyes can rotate independently, one in the opposite direction to the other; its tongue is protractile, which means it can hunt from afar, without needing to approach its prey. Like the god Apollo. Haven't you read *The Iliad*? Apollo, he who wounds from afar, that's how Homer keeps on referring to him. Let me confess something to you now, and believe me, I mean this with all my heart: if in another life I had to be an animal, do not doubt for even a second that this is the one I would be.

As you can see, the almost two years I have spent in my cell have also allowed me to write this novel; Iker didn't want to – you've got to be irresponsible to turn your nose up at an opportunity like the one I gave him, but it's his loss. In the end I've had to do it myself and it seems not to have turned out too bad at all, though you'll have to tell me what you think – if I ever decide to let you exist, that is, for there to be someone else on the other side of this story. Because if I don't, it's no big deal, I just destroy the book and all of you disappear. But I reckon I won't do that; when I get out of here I may well tap on a couple of keys and get this published, some time down the road perhaps, when things have calmed down. By then, I hope Laura Salinas will still be in prison, because her sentence was for fifteen years, four more than me, as I was never as close to the dead man as she was. So you see: the advantages of the chameleon.

And I hope too that Iker reconsiders. It hurts me that he has not come to see me even once in all this time, but maybe when I get out of here and I return to my life he'll be in a position to understand all that happened, and to realise that I never did anything that was not either because of him or for his sake. I bear him no grudge; in any case, he needs me. I have read his novel about the man who never appears in his own dreams, and I liked it, a couple of things could have done with some work possibly, but it's fine. I think the ending must be some kind of homage to Alcaén Sánchez, I mean the bit where the book's main character enters the room in which the vets put down the pigeons, sets the birds free and then gets inside the gas chamber, closes the door, shuts his eyes, the birds fly off into the sky, and as he starts to fall asleep, he has a dream that he is swimming in a pool. That's not bad, although personally I would have opted for something more intense; for example, that the man went on poisoning apples and reading the papers for news of his crimes; when people stopped buying fruit he started injecting the poison into bottles of water, and, when they started to drink water from the tap, he took to poisoning yoghurts, cartons of milk, juices . . . Oh well, it's just an idea, who's to say what's better or worse.

And now, if you'll excuse me, I have nothing more to tell you. I'm going to lie down and have a good sleep, like I do every day. Don't go thinking that I'm one of those who can't get to sleep at night, who stare into space, feel guilty in the midst of a darkness made all the worse by their remorse. I suppose Alcaén Sánchez must have felt something of the sort a few months ago, at the moment of his suicide, when he hung himself in his cell with the sheets from his bunk, poor fool. You're wrong if you think I feel no pity for him; I imagine him in that predicament, I see him hanging from the bars of the window, like a puppet tangled in its own strings, and I remember what Iker Orbáiz said, about how at the end of a rope there's always a noose. Although not for me, you can be certain of that.

Well, like I said, I'm off to sleep, I won't keep you any further. And you should go to bed as well. One day perhaps we'll meet again, maybe very soon. Who knows? I may well publish this novel and meet with great success. I may, from now on, become your favourite author. Until then, I'll bid you farewell, whoever you are, wherever you are.

And remember, lie on your right side. You must never sleep on your heart, because if you did, you would dream of the Devil.